That Alien Feeling

(Calluvia's Royalty #1)

Alessandra Hazard

D1718753

Table of Contents

That Alien Feeling

Chapter 1

Harry loved humans.

Everything about them was so fascinating. Even their names were refreshingly short and interesting, not at all like names back home.

Take Harry's name, for example.

Well, the point was, it wasn't his real name. His real name was very hard to pronounce for humans. The muscular properties of humans' tongues were limiting for certain types of phonetic articulation, including Harry's native language.

Harry liked his chosen human name better than his real one, anyway. "Harry" was similar enough to his given name and sounded so nice and unusual. He couldn't help but smile every time someone addressed him as Harry. Humans tended to give him strange looks when he beamed at them happily, but Harry didn't mind. He had read on the Internet that it was okay to be weird and quirky as long as one wasn't too weird. Hopefully he wasn't.

"Uh, dude, are you going to smile at me all day or are you going to finally give me my money?"

Torn from his musings, Harry smiled serenely at the big pink man who was frowning at him. (Harry didn't understand why humans called pink people "white" and brown people "black." Were humans color-blind? Humans were so confusing.)

"Sure thing, dude," Harry said, imitating the man's speech patterns. His research said that humans responded positively to mimicking their behavior. Harry was very good at it. He rather liked the man's accent.

The man's frown deepened. He looked at Harry oddly. "Are you mocking me?" He cracked his knuckles for some reason.

"No?" Harry said, bewildered, and gave him his change.

The man glowered at him, grabbed his coffee and his change, and left, the bell tinkling softly as he exited the coffee shop.

Harry worked at this little place called Star Coffee. He absolutely loved it! The apt name aside, it was quiet and charming, and it was also the only place willing to hire him. Harry had discovered that to survive on this planet he needed money, and the easiest way to make money was to find a job.

Unfortunately, he had also discovered that for a young human male without any education, job options were very limited. Harry was still a little angry at his parents for giving him only false identification documents with the name he'd chosen and a small amount of human money before dropping him in a city called London two Terran months ago.

"*It will teach you a lesson,*" they had told him. "*We've spoiled you too much. Maybe the experience will finally make you grow up.*"

Harry had been secretly pleased at the time. If his parents thought it was a punishment, they didn't know him at all. He'd always dreamed of getting off his planet and seeing the universe. Humans, or Terrans, as they called them back home, had always fascinated him. Their society hadn't yet reached the technological and cultural level required for Contact, but it wasn't long now, perhaps one thousand years at most unless humans destroyed themselves before that. For now, Earth was used only for short, educational trips—or when one's parents wanted to punish their child for doing naughty things like reading other people's minds without permission. (Harry had told his parents he didn't mean it, but, sadly, no one believed him.)

Anyway, having a real, human job was fascinating. Harry didn't mind working at Star Coffee. His boss had kindly agreed to give him his salary in cash and Harry didn't even mind that he seemed to earn less than the other employees. He took pride in the small stack of human money he received every month. There was no physical money on Calluvia anymore, hadn't been for a few thousand years.

Working at the coffee shop suited him very much. It was a job that wasn't suspicious for a young human male of eighteen years. That was his age according to his fake Terran documents. Harry wasn't actually eighteen; he was twenty-three in Calluvian years, but since a Calluvian year was shorter than a Terran year, he probably was around eighteen or nineteen in Terran years.

Harry wasn't sure; mathematics had never been his strongest point.

"Hey."

Torn from his daydreaming once again, Harry looked at the next customer.

It was a young male in a dark suit. His skin wasn't as pink as the previous man's. It was more golden than pink. He had very dark, very nice eyes. Harry liked dark eyes. They were so rare on Calluvia, unlike Harry's own violet eyes.

"Hello," Harry said, flashing the human a friendly smile. He had learned that humans gave bigger tips when he did that. Harry felt a little bad for exploiting it, but a guy's gotta eat, as humans said.

The human smiled back, handing him a five-pound note. "A cappuccino, please."

When Harry returned with his coffee, the guy said, "Thank you, Harry."

"Oh!" Harry said, beaming at him. "How do you know my name?"

The human gave him an odd look. "It's on your nametag."

"Oh," Harry said, flushing. How embarrassing.

The guy's smile widened, something like amusement flickering in his eyes. Harry wanted to know the human's thoughts so badly he had to dig his fingers into his palms to distract himself. *Bad, bad Harry,* he scolded himself. His parents wouldn't be amused if they found out that he was exploiting his telepathy again. (Harry never had bad intentions. He just had a curious mind. Literally.)

"Keep the change, love," the man said.

Harry decided that he liked this human. He liked all humans, really, but this one was very nice. Maybe he would make a good friend.

Harry brightened at the thought. He had wanted to make friends since his arrival, but in the first few weeks he hadn't been confident enough in his ability to pass for a human and hadn't dared. Perhaps it was time to try. Harry was positive he made a very convincing human. Sure, people thought he was odd, but no one ever suspected the truth.

"What is your name?" Harry said enthusiastically.

The human's dark eyebrows lifted a little. "Adam," he said.

"Really?" Harry said, pleased that he knew something about the name and there wouldn't be awkward silences in the conversation. "That's what the first human was called!"

Adam stared at him.

Harry deflated a little. Had he gotten it wrong?

"Yes," Adam said after a beat. "Sort of."

Relieved, Harry smiled brighter. "Have you found your Eve yet?"

Adam blinked and cocked his head to the side, eyeing Harry. "Not exactly," he said at last. "I don't swing that way I'm afraid."

Harry frowned, confused once again. His translating chip must have been malfunctioning. Adam didn't look afraid, and Harry didn't understand what a swing had to do with Adam's relationship status. "Swing that way?" he said, hoping his confusion didn't seem too odd.

"Are you a foreigner?" Adam said, chuckling softly.

Harry nodded, pleased that there was a plausible explanation for his ignorance.

"Odd," Adam said. "You don't have an accent."

"I'm very good at accents," Harry said honestly. His translating chip could only get him so far. It didn't help him much with accents and slang. "So what did you mean?"

"I meant that I don't like women that way. I'm afraid there's no Eve for me."

"Oh," Harry breathed. When Adam started frowning, he grinned. "This is so cool! I've never met a homosexual person in my life!"

"I doubt it. You probably have, just didn't realize. We look just like heterosexuals. So inconsiderate of us."

Adam had said it seriously, but Harry wasn't fooled.

He pouted. "Yeah, make fun of a foreigner struggling with your culture and language."

Adam laughed, lightly tapping Harry on the nose. "Sorry, couldn't resist—you're adorable, kid."

Harry scrunched his nose up. "I'm not a kid. I'm tw— eighteen."

"Well, I'm twenty-six," Adam said, glancing at his watch. "And I have to go."

Harry frowned. "Already?"

He couldn't quite hide his disappointment, and Adam smiled at him. "Are you disappointed?"

"Yes," Harry said.

Adam chuckled. "My lunch break is almost over."

"What's your job?"

"I'm a financial analyst at the bank on the other side of the street," Adam said with a smile that made Harry suspect he was humoring him.

"That sounds interesting," Harry said.

"Not really," Adam said. "But it pays well, and I suppose I can't complain. I really have to go. It was nice to meet you, Harry."

"Likewise," Harry said earnestly. "Come here again!"

"I will," Adam said before reaching out and touching the flower tucked behind Harry's ear. "You know, on any other bloke this would look weird, but it suits you."

Harry beamed at him. "Thanks!" He liked the way the purple flower looked in his chestnut hair. It almost made his eyes seem purple.

Harry watched a little sadly as Adam took his coffee and left.

He hoped it wasn't the last he'd see of him.

* * *

Adam did return to the coffee shop two days later. He wasn't alone this time.

Harry watched curiously as Adam and his companion talked, sipping their drinks. He hadn't been the one to take their order—Samantha had while he was on a break—and now Harry was left floundering. Should he go say hi? Adam hadn't looked his way even once yet. Maybe he didn't remember Harry.

"What's with that sad face, Hazza?" Samantha said.

Hazza. Human nicknames were fascinating.

Harry told her about his dilemma. "Should I go say hi?"

Samantha looked back at the pair. "Better not. Maybe they're on a date."

"A date?"

Samantha shrugged. "Yeah. They're both hot, and they look pretty cozy to me."

Bewildered, Harry returned his gaze to Adam and his male companion. They did seem rather cozy. Adam's companion was a young dark-skinned man, who possessed a symmetrical face with symmetrical features, which was universally considered beautiful. But Harry wasn't sure of the man's sexual appeal the way humans would just know. Sometimes the differences between their species were so frustrating.

"Do you think Adam's date is attractive?" Harry said. Adam was his friend (hopefully). Harry wanted him to be happy.

Samantha shrugged again. "He's very good-looking. Though, in my opinion, your Adam is still out of his league." She smiled wryly. "Your Adam is out of most people's league."

Harry smiled. He knew what that expression meant!

"You think so?" he said, trying to look at Adam objectively. But it was so difficult. Calluvian sexuality was very different from that of humans. The closest human sexuality he could think of was demisexuality, and that wasn't entirely accurate, either. Until Harry's childhood bond to his betrothed became a marriage bond when he turned twenty-five in two years, his sex drive would be non-existent, and even then he would be attracted only to his bondmate.

Well, there were whispers that sometimes people had sex outside of a bond, but Harry thought it was preposterous. Everyone knew that your bondmate completed you, and that the telepathic link made sex perfect. Calluvians had been practicing marriage bonds for thousands of years. It was scientifically proven that a bond was superior to the way things had been done in the past. Every Calluvian child was bonded telepathically to another and grew up knowing their bondmate from a very early age. Harry thought it was very smart.

But now it presented a problem, since Harry couldn't really see humans the way other humans did.

Harry could see that Adam, with his tall, athletic figure, dark hair and dark eyes was aesthetically pleasing to the eye, but he couldn't properly judge his sexual appeal. Heck, Harry didn't know what sex *was*, or rather, he knew only theoretically.

"Yeah, he's a hottie," Samantha said with a dreamy sigh. "That chiseled jaw... that stubble... that dark smolder... mmm...Yummy!"

Harry burst out laughing. At moments like this, he was so glad he couldn't make a fool out of himself because of things like lust. It seemed so ridiculous to him.

His laughter made Adam turn his head. Adam nodded to him with a smile. Harry waved cheerfully. Adam's smile widened, turning amused and... something else. He said something to his companion and made his way to the counter.

"Hey, Harry," he said, leaning forward against the counter. Harry would worry for his immaculate suit, but he knew the counter was spotlessly clean. He had cleaned it himself.

"Hi there!" Harry said. "How is your date going?"

Adam snorted. "Jake isn't a date. He's my friend and colleague. Do you think I'm such a cheap date that I'd bring my date to this coffee shop?"

"Hey," Harry drawled with a pout.

Adam smirked. "Just kidding, babe. This is a first-rate establishment. Anyone would be honored to be brought here on a date."

Harry nodded importantly. "Exactly." Babe. Adam had called him a babe. It was a little odd, because he wasn't an infant, but Harry knew by now that humans often didn't mean things in the literal sense. Babe. He decided he rather liked being called "babe."

Remembering that he was supposed to be working, he said, "Did you want something?"

"Not really," Adam said, glancing back at his friend, who was watching them with raised eyebrows. "Just came over to say hi."

Harry beamed at him. "Hi yourself. I've been just thinking about you, actually—wondering if you'd come again. I liked you very much and hoped we could be friends."

Adam stared at him for a moment. "You haven't a coy bone in your body, do you?" he murmured, shaking his head, but his eyes were smiling. "Okay, give me your phone, I'll give you my number."

Harry deflated. "I don't have a mobile phone," he admitted in a small voice. Even he knew how unusual and strange the lack of a mobile phone was for a human.

Adam blinked. "Really?"

Harry nodded.

He supposed he could lie and tell Adam that he'd lost his phone, but he hated lying and wasn't very good at it.

"I don't really know many people in this country, so I never got around to buying one." Harry shrugged with an embarrassed smile. "I don't really have spare money for one, anyway."

Adam's brows drew together. "Are you an orphan?"

"No!" Harry said quickly, the mere thought of his parents' death upsetting him greatly. "My parents are back home. They're normally very supportive, it's just..." He chewed on his lip. "I did something bad and they got angry with me. They said I should learn how to be a responsible adult, so they kind of cut me off. Don't look at me that way. It's just temporary. They'll get over it. They love me. I'm their youngest—the baby of the family."

Smiling, Adam pinched his cheek. "That I can believe."

Unthinkingly, Harry touched his hand—

You're the most endearing thing I've ever met.

Oh, no.

Harry really didn't mean to. He didn't! He'd just forgotten that humans, as non-telepathic species, were completely unprotected against touch-telepathy—the simplest form of telepathy that could be blocked by a basic mental shield that even kids mastered easily back home. But he wasn't home. He had no right to violate humans' privacy by eavesdropping on their thoughts. His parents would be so mad at him if they found out.

"Sorry," Harry said, withdrawing his fingers and balling them behind his back. However, he couldn't help but feel pleased that Adam thought he was endearing. It meant they were friends, right?

"Anyway!" he said, ignoring the odd look Adam was giving him. "If you aren't dating Jake, where's your second half?"

Adam said, "Nowhere. I'm married to my job I'm afraid."

"That's too bad," Harry said, sad on Adam's behalf. He knew humans were social beings. "Everyone needs a strong emotional bond."

Adam gave him an amused look. "You sound like my old grandma. And how many emotional bonds have you had, oh wise one?"

"You're mocking me." Harry pouted. "I'll have you know I already know the person I'm going to be with for the rest of my life."

Adam's amused smile slipped off. "That's a very serious statement coming from an eighteen-year-old," he said after a moment. "And who's the lucky girl?"

"Her name is..." Harry hesitated for a moment. He hated lying, but there was no way he could give Adam his bondmate's real name—Leylen'shni'gul—for the same reason he couldn't give his. So he chose one that sounded close enough in a Terran language. "Her name is Leyla. We've known each other practically all our lives."

"Wow," Adam said, a wrinkle appearing on his forehead. "And you love her so much you're sure you'll be with her all your life?"

Harry suppressed a sigh. It was very hard to explain how the bond worked to a human.

"We share a special bond," Harry said tentatively. They did. He and his bondmate had been bonded since they were two years old.

"She's always in my thoughts and I'm in hers." Harry smiled, pleased that he hadn't lied once so far. They did have a telepathic connection, though he couldn't feel it on Earth because of the physical distance between them. "We're engaged and... will be married in two years," he added, proud that he'd found human equivalents to the state of his bond.

Adam smiled faintly. "That's very young to marry."

Harry shrugged. "Not really. That's the age people marry back home."

"And where would that home be?" Adam said. "You haven't told me where you are from."

Harry froze for a moment before remembering the advice his best friend had given him: *"If they ask, just tell Terrans you're an alien. They'll never believe you and will just think you're being funny."*

Harry said conversationally, "I'm actually an alien from the star system in the Sagittarius constellation."

"Ah," Adam said with a smile. "That explains your creepy alien eyes."

"What! What's wrong with my eyes?"

Adam shot him a strange look. "They're dark violet color, Harry. Surely you realize that's pretty unusual?"

The corners of Harry's mouth turned down. Why had no one told him that his eyes weren't very human? He could have worn colored contact lenses. He'd seen an advertisement on the TV.

"Hey," Adam said, tipping Harry's face up with his thumb. He was frowning. "Are you upset? Don't be silly. Your eyes are very beautiful—unusual but beautiful."

Blushing, Harry smiled at him. "You're so nice to me! I like you a lot. Would you like to be my friend? I'd love to have you as my friend."

Adam chuckled. "How are you even real?" he murmured, brushing his thumb over Harry's cheek. "Yes, I would love to be your friend, love."

Harry beamed at him, warmth and happiness filling his chest as he looked into Adam's smiling dark eyes. He missed this—having a connection to another person. It might not be telepathic, as he was used to, but it felt good. For the first time since his arrival on Earth, Harry admitted to himself that he had been a little lonely here. Just a little.

But not anymore.

Chapter 2

"Hey," Helene said, sticking her head into Adam's office. "I'm about to head out. I'm going to that little Italian place around the corner. "Wanna go with me?"

"Yep," Jake said. "I'm starving. Missed lunch today."

"Sorry, can't," Adam said, turning off his computer.

Jake snorted. "Adam has a very important meeting at that coffee shop across the street."

Adam shot him an unimpressed look and grabbed the box from his desk before heading out.

But Jake was undeterred. "Seriously, man," he said, catching up to Adam. "Why don't you just ask the kid out? What's stopping you? Sure, he's almost jailbait, but it's not like it's illegal or something. I'm already sick of watching you eat him with your eyes. It's nauseating."

"I don't eat him with my eyes," Adam said.

"Please. I saw you all but drooling the other day when the kid smiled at you. If you were a dog, you would have been wagging your tail and licking all over his face."

Adam sighed through his gritted teeth. "Let it go, Jake. Harry is a friend, that's all. Nothing can come out of it."

"Why not?"

Adam bit out, "Because he's straight and engaged."

And it wasn't the only reason.

Harry was... too good for someone like him. Harry was such a sunshine, everything good, happy, and kind, everything he could ever want all rolled into one person. Adam sometimes had to pinch himself to make sure he hadn't dreamed Harry up: he was one of those rare people who were beautiful inside and out.

It's just a stupid crush, he told himself. A stupid juvenile crush on a *boy*. Harry might have been legal, but sometimes he seemed so naive and innocent that it made Adam want to wrap Harry in his arms and hide him from the cruel, dirty world. *He* was dirty, too, because despite all the affection and protectiveness he felt for the strange boy, he still wanted. Wanted to bury himself in Harry's sweetness and dirty him up with his greedy hands and mouth, fuck him up and ruin him. Adam felt like a bloody pervert for wanting that, because Harry genuinely thought they were friends. And they were. Of course they were. It wasn't Harry's fault that he wanted more.

"Sorry, man," Jake said, clapping him on the shoulder.

Adam just shrugged. He didn't want to talk about it.

Bidding his goodbye to Jake, Adam headed to the familiar coffee shop across the street.

The bell chimed cheerfully as he pushed the door open. Harry looked up and smiled at him. Adam smiled back and walked toward the counter.

The coffee shop was pretty busy that evening and there were a couple of customers in front of him. Adam took the opportunity to watch Harry while he served the others.

Harry had his chestnut hair brushed back that evening. His porcelain skin looked as flawless and soft as usual. His violet eyes were kind and attentive as Harry listened to the elderly woman in front of him, his pink lips quick to smile when she tipped him generously. Adam could relate. Lately he spent more money in this little coffee shop than was probably healthy.

The elderly woman finally said her goodbyes, and two little girls, twins about six, stepped forward, pointing excitedly at the chocolate cake.

"Give us the cake, please," they said together and started emptying their pockets to reveal what was probably the total of their savings, coins rolling everywhere, even on the floor.

Harry beamed down at the little girls, looking utterly charmed instead of annoyed as he started counting the coins. "Is it your birthday?"

The girls shook their heads. "We just like chocolate," one of them said.

"And cake," the other said.

"So we're killing two birds with one stone," the first one imparted with an important look.

Harry blinked at them.

Adam could tell he was a little confused—he probably didn't know that idiom either—but Harry smiled widely despite his confusion and gave them the cake. "Here it is, loves."

Adam could tell the girls' money was nowhere near enough for the cake and tried not to feel utterly charmed as Harry pulled some money out of his pocket and added it to the little girls' coins.

The next customer was a guy about Harry's age.

"Sorry, buddy, but what are you wearing?" he said with a laugh.

Harry frowned a little and looked down at himself. Adam smiled slightly. In the past three weeks since he had met Harry, he had gotten used to Harry's quirks, and he'd stopped noticing how oddly Harry dressed. It was a good thing the coffee shop owner didn't seem to believe in uniforms.

This day he was wearing a pair of old jeans and an oversized shirt under his apron. The shirt was bright orange with splashes of green and blue. It was truly hideous, but on Harry it somehow looked cute.

"I don't understand," Harry told the customer, blinking.

The guy snorted. "I wouldn't be caught dead in that orange thing you're wearing. Hell, even my grandma wouldn't be caught dead wearing it!"

Adam felt a wave of irritation at the guy when Harry's face fell.

"Oh," Harry said, touching his shirt. "I bought it with my first salary."

"Sorry, but it's hideous," the guy said. "Black coffee, please."

Harry silently served him and said goodbye with a polite smile.

"It isn't," Adam said the moment they were alone. "It's not hideous, Haz. You look lovely in it."

Harry smiled at him and stroked the fabric of his shirt again. "You don't have to lie," he said, waving his hand dismissively. "I know my tastes seem weird and... yeah." He grabbed a rag and wiped the spotless counter.

"Hey," Adam said, putting a hand on Harry's shoulder. When Harry looked at him, Adam said, "I'm not lying, babe. Fuck that idiot. The shirt is a bit of an eyesore, to be honest, but you're totally rocking it."

Harry laughed, his eyes finally brightening. "It's very soft," he admitted. "That's why I bought it. But I didn't think the color was terrible or anything. I love it. It cheers me up on gray, rainy days and there are lots of days like that!"

"As long as you love it, screw what everyone else thinks," Adam said. "But for all it's worth, I think you look great." *You always do.*

Harry chuckled. "Thanks." He handed Adam his usual order. "Anything else?"

"Yes, actually." Adam put the box he'd brought from his office on the counter. "This is for you."

Harry looked from the box to Adam, surprise on his face. "For me? Like, a present?"

"Yes," Adam replied.

Harry looked at the calendar on the wall, his brows furrowed a little. "I didn't know this was an occasion for giving presents," he said uncertainly.

"It isn't." Adam shrugged. "I just like giving presents to all my friends, no reason required," he lied, hoping Harry wouldn't tell Jake about this; he'd never hear the end of it. Adam could almost hear Jake's mocking. *Where's my present, Crawford?*

"Oh," Harry said, chewing on his lip. "But I don't have a present for you."

"It doesn't matter, Hazza," Adam said. "Come on, open it while there are no customers."

"Actually, we're supposed to be closed already," Harry said, walking to the door and locking it. He returned to the counter, face bright with excitement as he grabbed the box. It shouldn't have been so endearing, Jesus.

Adam watched Harry open the box carefully and examine its contents.

"It's a mobile phone," Harry said after a moment, with a strange expression on his face.

"I hope you like it."

"I do," Harry said softly. He looked at the label and pursed his lips, hesitation flickering in his eyes. "But isn't it expensive? I think I've seen this one on the TV."

As Samsung's latest model of its flagship phone, it certainly wasn't cheap, but Harry didn't need to know that.

"Don't worry, it didn't put a dent in my savings," Adam said. It wasn't a lie. He didn't have many people to spend his money on. He did help his parents financially, but they lived in the countryside and insisted that they didn't need much, so his bank account was comfortably full.

Harry gave him a look. "I'm not an idiot, Adam. I know this phone isn't cheap. I can't accept it."

He looked so endearingly stubborn that Adam wanted to kiss the little frown between his brows and then his pursed pink lips.

Adam suppressed a grimace. He had it so bad it wasn't funny anymore.

"I can't return it," he said. "And I already have a mobile phone. I guess I wasted money for nothing."

Harry laughed. "You're terrible, you know that, right?" Harry stepped closer and kissed him gently on the cheek. "Thank you so much. Really. Now I can be like every normal human!"

"You're such an oddball," Adam said fondly, telling himself his cheek wasn't tingling from the innocent contact. He wasn't that pathetic.

"I am." Harry turned the phone on with the cutest look of great concentration on his face. Sometimes Adam thought that, wherever Harry's home was, it couldn't be very technologically advanced—Harry constantly seemed tentative and unsure around all sorts of technological gadgets. Adam had tried numerous times to ask about Harry's home, but Harry just repeated the same answer he'd given him the first time—that he was an alien—before laughing and changing the subject. It made Adam wonder. It was strange for an eighteen-year-old to live in another country seemingly without any support or supervision. But he didn't push. Harry would talk when he was ready.

"Can I have your number?" Harry said with a pleased smile, as though he got a kick out of saying it.

"I've already put it in there," Adam said. "So you can call or text me whenever you want."

Harry blinked rapidly before nodding and turning away. "I was wondering..." he said haltingly. "Are you free now? Would you like to come to my place, watch a movie or something? I got Netflix yesterday! We could Netflix and chill?"

Adam choked on his coffee and started coughing.

Harry was by his side immediately. "Are you okay?" he said, patting Adam on the back. Harry's face was completely innocent. Of course it was. Harry had no clue.

Adam cleared his throat, loosening his tie a little. "Fine."

"So what about Netflix?"

He should say no. He really shouldn't spend more time with this straight, taken, *engaged* bloke. It was positively masochistic.

But Harry was looking at him with such a hopeful expression, his violet eyes big and earnest, and fuck, this kid had him completely wrapped around his little finger already.

"Okay," Adam said. "But...You really need to look up what 'Netflix and chill' means. Wouldn't want people to get the wrong idea, Haz."

Five minutes later, Harry emerged from the back room, his face scarlet red.

"Ready to go?" Adam said, pulling out his car keys.

Harry just nodded.

"I asked Samantha what 'Netflix and chill' meant," he said when he took the passenger seat in Adam's car. "I'm so embarrassed."

Adam snorted, starting the engine. "You're lucky you made the mistake with me and not anyone else. Someone else would think you were leading them on."

Harry chuckled, pressing his hands against his flushed cheeks. "Good thing I have you to tell me when I'm being a dumb foreigner."

"Well, you did tell me you were an alien. For an alien, your grasp of English is excellent."

"Thank you," Harry said with an expression Adam couldn't quite read.

"So where's your place?" Adam asked.

Harry gave him the address and Adam entered it into the navigation system.

The drive didn't take long. Twenty minutes later, Harry was letting him into his flat.

Adam's first impression was the tiny size of the place. The flat consisted of a tiny kitchen and a tiny room that was barely big enough to accommodate an old brown couch, a small coffee table, and a TV. There was no bed. Adam looked at the short, hard couch and suppressed a grimace as he imagined Harry sleeping on it. It looked more than a little uncomfortable.

"It's not much," Harry said, looking a little self-conscious.

"You should have seen my first flat in London," Adam said with a chuckle, sitting down on the couch. It was as uncomfortable as it looked. "It was bigger, but I had three flatmates."

"I'll get popcorn. Pick something to watch?"

Adam hummed in agreement and Harry left the room, disappearing into the kitchen.

Adam looked around, a little unsettled. The flat was downright claustrophobic.

But he said nothing when Harry returned with a bowl of popcorn and two Diet Cokes. Harry looked so excited and pleased. Adam didn't want to ruin his mood by making him feel embarrassed. The rent was expensive in London. It was admirable that Harry managed to get by on his own.

Harry plopped next to Adam and spread a blanket over their laps, placing the bowl with popcorn between them.

Adam closed his eyes for a moment. It was a struggle to keep his body relaxed. The couch was too fucking small.

"Why didn't you pick a movie?" Harry said.

"I wanted you to."

"Okay, but no complaining if you don't like it!"

Adam watched Harry browse Netflix, trying to suppress the urge to put an arm around Harry's shoulders and pull him even closer.

In an attempt to distract himself, he picked up the stack of DVDs from the coffee table and raised his eyebrows when he saw the titles. "You're interested in sci-fi?"

Was Harry blushing?

"Samantha is a big science fiction fan," Harry said. "She loaned me a couple of movies that weren't on Netflix. They looked interesting."

"I didn't think *War of the Worlds* was the kind of movie you would enjoy. It's pretty violent and gross." Harry had mentioned he didn't like violence in movies.

Harry scowled at the DVD in Adam's hand. "I didn't like it very much. The plot didn't make sense to me. It's ridiculous that aliens would want to invade Earth. What for? There are millions of planets without sentient life!"

Adam stared at him in mild surprise. "I didn't know you felt so passionately about it," he said, a little amused. "Do you really believe in aliens, Haz?"

Harry looked at him. "You don't?"

Adam shrugged. "Never really thought about it."

He smoothed the wrinkle between Harry's brows with his thumb. "But who knows. I think it's statistically impossible that intelligent life could develop only on Earth when there are billions of stars out there. It would be pretty arrogant of us to think so."

Harry nodded. "Intelligent life is pretty rare in the universe—" He paused. "I mean, I believe it's pretty rare," he corrected himself, dropping his gaze. "But it can't be that rare, right? There are a hundred billion stars in this galaxy alone. Sure, not all stars have planets, and not all of them are habitable, but the odds are still very good that there are thousands of intelligent civilizations only in this galaxy."

"But how many of them would be around long enough to develop interstellar travel?" Adam murmured, fascinated by the fire in Harry's eyes. For some reason, Harry really felt strongly about the subject.

"True," Harry said, nodding. "The truth is, many civilizations would destroy themselves if their technological level becomes high enough." Harry popped a piece of popcorn into his mouth. "Anyway, enough about it!" he said, grabbing another DVD. "What about this one? I think it's a sequel to the movie I watched yesterday. I liked it very much."

"Hmm, I have seen the first movie, but not the sequel," Adam said.

That was how they ended up watching *Star Trek into Darkness.*

The movie was okay, but then again, Adam spent most of the movie watching Harry and listening to his commentary, so he couldn't be all that sure.

"This Prime Directive thing makes so much sense," Harry said at some point.

"Interfering into another civilization's natural development is a really bad idea. It can have really unfortunate consequences. I don't understand why Spock would even go along with that mad plan in the first place."

Adam chuckled, brushing his fingers over Harry's cheek. "Babe, it's just a movie. Don't take it so seriously. Aliens aren't real, remember? Well, maybe they are, but we haven't met them yet."

Harry looked at him with wide eyes before laughing awkwardly. "I'm an alien, remember?"

Adam rolled his eyes with a fond smile and they returned to watching the movie.

But soon, Adam noticed that Harry had grown very quiet. Adam squeezed Harry's shoulder. "Hey, you okay?"

Harry was chewing on his lip, his gaze far away and thoughtful. Adam had rarely seen him so somber.

"Do you think lying is ever okay?"

Adam frowned, puzzled by the random question. "I think it depends on circumstances," he said, eyeing Harry. "Sometimes lying is the best option."

Harry nodded. He still wouldn't look at Adam.

"What's wrong, love?" Adam said.

Harry swallowed and forced a faint smile. "Never mind me. I've been in a weird mood lately. I guess I'm just homesick. I've never been away from home for so long." He smiled crookedly. "I guess I'm really a baby." He glanced around the tiny room. "I love it here, but it gets lonely, you know? It's a little scary to be on my own. Until I got here, I barely made any decisions in my life and now I'm making them every day. But you know the weirdest thing? I like it. I think I'm going to miss the freedom of making my own decisions. It won't be possible at home."

Adam stared at his bowed head. The more he learned about Harry's home, the less he liked it. "Haz," he said. "Is…your home situation okay?"

Harry blinked before laughing. "It's not that bad. My life back home is very… comfortable and peaceful. I don't have to work a day of my life if I don't want to. I mean, certain things are expected from me, but I'm not obliged to do most of them. My family adores me, and I adore them, too." Harry sighed. "I miss them very much." Harry tapped on his new phone idly. "I like it here, but until I met you, I felt kind of lonely. I miss having… connections to people. Now I kind of get why my parents chose this as a punishment." He chuckled wetly. "You shouldn't have given me this phone. It's your own fault if I bother you every time I feel lonely in my head."

"You can bother me whenever you want, Haz," Adam said, studying him. He'd never seen him so down. "Hey. Do you want a hug?"

Harry blinked at him. "A hug?"

Smiling, Adam opened his arms. "Come here."

Harry bit his lip before moving and curling in Adam's lap.

Adam went still. This definitely wasn't what he'd had in mind.

After a moment, he wrapped his arms around Harry's back and squeezed, hoping he radiated only comfort and friendly reassurance and didn't seem like a possessive creep who wanted to take this boy inside his skin and hide him from the world. *Mine.*

"Mmm," Harry murmured, burying his face in the crook of Adam's neck. "This feels good. No one has hugged me since I was a small child."

Adam's forehead creased. "What?" Honestly, the more he learned about Harry's home, the more concerned he got. "What about your parents?"

Harry didn't say anything for a while. "Things are different back home," he said. "We prefer... spiritual closeness back home rather than physical."

Adam snorted. "You sound like a bunch of hippies."

"Hey!" Harry said. "What's wrong with being a hippie?"

"Nothing," Adam said, stroking Harry's back and allowing himself to bury his nose in Harry's hair. It smelled of something sweet. *Mineminemine.*

Adam managed to shove the creepy, possessive thoughts out of his mind, but his arms still tightened around Harry until there was no space left between them. Harry made a pleased noise, pressing deeper into him and generally acting like a clingy monkey. He seemed touch-starved. It was no wonder if he hadn't been hugged in years.

Adam dropped a kiss on top of Harry's head, affection washing over him, overwhelming in its intensity.

And then came fear.

Because the young man curled in his arms wasn't his, no matter how badly he wanted it. There was something about Harry that seemed unreal, as if one day Harry would disappear from his life as suddenly as he had entered it.

Chapter 3

Harry had told Adam the truth: it had been years since anyone had hugged him. He remembered being hugged as a kid, but as he grew up, his family had started giving him space, as it was custom. Back home, hugging was considered an invasion of one's privacy, since physical touch increased the chance of telepathic transference.

Harry must have forgotten how good it felt, because it quickly became Harry's favorite thing in the world. He was a little embarrassed by how much he wanted it, but Adam didn't seem to mind that Harry was constantly all over his personal space, wanting to be hugged and cuddled. At first, hugging had been just a substitute for the glaring absence of his telepathic links to his family and bondmate, but by this point, Harry was afraid he was more than a little addicted to it.

Adam was an amazing hugger. Harry felt warm, cherished, and adored every time Adam's strong body surrounded his own. It was amazing, really, how a simple hug could make him feel so much better, putting a spring in Harry's step for most of the day.

The only downside was, Harry had had to work hard on strengthening his mental shields, careful not to read Adam's mind without his permission. Harry was no saint. He'd always been naturally curious, and he was really, really curious about what Adam thought of him, but he didn't want to exploit his telepathy. It felt dishonest. Adam didn't deserve that.

"Is your boyfriend coming today?" Samantha said, tearing him away from his thoughts.

Harry looked at her with a small frown. "What?"

Samantha grinned. "Come on, Haz, don't play coy. I'm not stupid!"

"I don't understand," Harry said slowly. "What are you talking about?"

Samantha rolled her eyes. "Tall, dark, and handsome, comes here every day like clockwork? Gives you obscenely big tips? Ring any bells?"

Harry laughed. "Adam? Don't be silly, he's not my boyfriend! He's a friend."

Samantha stared at him. "Are you pulling my leg?"

Harry swallowed his confusion—he didn't understand what pulling Samantha's leg had to do with the conversation, but the context was pretty clear, so he didn't ask—and said, "No, I'm not. I'm serious. Adam's my best friend. I have a—fiancée back home." Not to mention that Calluvians didn't have boyfriends or girlfriends. They had bondmates, and Adam obviously wasn't his.

Samantha looked at him oddly. "Harry, you sit in his lap when there are no other customers," she intoned.

Harry's frown deepened.

"So?" he said defensively. "I like it and Adam doesn't mind!"

Samantha's expression turned skeptical. "Look, I'm all for men expressing their emotions and being comfortable with physical touch—it's the twenty-first century—but you have to admit it looks pretty strange when you sit in his lap for half an hour and cling to him like a baby koala."

Harry pursed his lips, starting to get upset. "Are you implying it's not normal for friends in this country?"

"It really isn't," Samantha said with a pinched look. "I'm sorry, but how can you be so socially inept, Haz?"

Harry looked down, picking at a brownie on the plate in front of him. He hated feeling so stupid and socially awkward. He had friends back home and he certainly didn't hug them— adults didn't hug each other on Calluvia—but he thought it was normal for humans. Adam was his only friend here. How was he supposed to know their friendship was strange by human standards? Why hadn't Adam told him that Harry was behaving weirdly and was being too clingy for a friend? Harry knew Adam had a soft spot for him, but surely that wouldn't stop him from telling Harry to be less of a weird idiot?

"I didn't know," Harry muttered, his mood ruined. He had been so looking forward to the end of his shift— Adam usually showed up around that time, too—and now he kind of dreaded it, horribly embarrassed.

Why didn't Adam tell him?

The question bothered him for the rest of his shift.

When he heard the chime of the bell as his shift neared its end, Harry didn't need to turn around to know it was Adam. He knew, somehow.

Harry took a few deep breaths, trying to fight the feeling of mortification and failing.

"Hey, babe," Adam said.

Reluctantly, Harry turned around.

The easy smile on Adam's lips faded. "All right, Haz?"

Normally, at this point, Harry would approach him, put his head on Adam's shoulder and lean against him, silently asking for a hug. Adam would oblige, securing his arms around Harry, and they would talk for a while, discussing their respective days, or just chat about everything and nothing. Harry hadn't realized how weird it was—or how much he wanted it until he couldn't do it anymore.

"Why didn't you tell me I was being a terrible friend?" Harry said.

Adam's expression didn't change. "What?"

"Samantha told me friends don't hug so much," Harry said, lowering his gaze to the counter. "That I'm too clingy."

Silence.

Then Adam rounded the counter and tipped Harry's face up with his fingers. "Hey, don't be silly. You're not a terrible friend. I'm more than happy to hug you if that's what you want."

Harry's stomach dropped. "But what about what you want?"

A strange look flickered over Adam's face. "I happen to enjoy hugging." He chuckled, his teeth flashing. "Did you really think I was just putting up with it? I have too little patience for that."

"But you don't hug Jake at all and he's your friend, too," Harry pointed out, suddenly realizing that he'd never seen Adam hug Jake.

Adam raised his eyebrows. "How do you know?

"Maybe we cuddle all the time when you don't see us."

An unfamiliar, unpleasant feeling settled low in Harry's stomach. He wasn't sure what it was, but he didn't like it. "Do you?" he said, trying not to think of Jake wrapped in Adam's arms. It felt wrong, somehow.

Adam snorted. "No. Jake would think I'm mad if I tried to snuggle him up."

Good. He didn't want Adam to hold anyone but him.

"See?" Harry said, confused by his own thoughts. Where was this proprietary feeling coming from? He'd always been good at sharing.

Adam gave him a long, unreadable look. "Harry, if you want me to stop hugging you, just say it."

"No," Harry said, grabbing Adam's tie and playing with it nervously. "Please don't stop—but as long as you want it, too."

Adam smiled at him—that soft, slightly crooked smile that he seemed to reserve just for Harry—and said, "I do."

Harry smiled a little and, looping his arms around Adam's neck, leaned his cheek against Adam's shoulder. He sighed happily when Adam's hard, muscular arms wrapped tightly around him, making him feel warm, safe, and so, so good. It was such an addictive feeling.

Harry loosened Adam's tie, unbuttoned the top button of Adam's shirt and tucked his face against Adam's throat, taking deep, greedy breaths. He loved Adam's scent so much. He wished he could bottle it up and put it on his pillow so he could sleep better.

He hummed in pleasure when Adam's strong fingers massaged his nape and his shoulder blades—they ached a little after his long shift.

Sometimes he thought Adam was a telepath, too. Adam always seemed to know what he needed.

"Are you free?" Harry mumbled, nuzzling at Adam's throat with his eyes closed. "Movie night? Want?" It was a little embarrassing how incoherent he got when they snuggled.

Adam seemed to find it amusing and had told Harry he was just touch-starved. Harry wasn't that sure about it, but either way, it was embarrassing.

Adam sighed.

"Sorry, Haz, can't."

"Why not?" Harry said, his dreams of spending a blissful couple of hours snuggled up against Adam shattering into a thousand pieces.

"Got a date tonight," Adam said.

Harry opened his eyes. "A date?" he repeated. "With whom?"

"Someone I met through work," Adam said, letting his arms fall and stepping away from Harry. "I need to go home and change now or I'll be late, actually."

"Oh," Harry said, suddenly feeling cold. "Don't let me keep you."

"See you tomorrow," Adam said, brushing his lips against Harry's temple. "Bye, babe."

"Bye," Harry said without his usual cheer. He didn't understand why his mood plummeted.

He returned to his flat an hour later and sat down in front of the TV.

Harry normally loved it—he found human technology charmingly old-fashioned if at times frustrating—but this night he couldn't quite summon interest for anything on the TV.

Sighing, Harry went to the kitchen and got some ice cream out of the freezer. Adam had implied that humans ate ice cream when they felt down, and it supposedly helped. Harry grabbed a spoon too, returned to the couch, and dug in.

Half an hour later, the ice cream was gone, but Harry didn't feel particularly better, just uncomfortably full. Either ice cream worked only on humans, or he had misunderstood Adam. The latter still happened quite often.

Harry picked up the remote and started channel surfing. But nothing could hold his interest, and after an hour, he gave up and decided to go to sleep. He didn't feel like eating, still full from the ice cream.

The couch felt more uncomfortable than usual, creaking every time he shifted.

Harry wondered whether he should find another, better-paying job so he could afford a better flat, but he loved the coffee shop. Besides, Adam's office was next to the coffee shop.

The thought of Adam made Harry's stomach churn uncomfortably and he forced himself to change the direction of his thoughts.

Harry thought of home, of his parents and siblings. He'd been on Earth months already. Without Adam's presence, Harry couldn't ignore the loud silence at the back of his mind. He hadn't known silence could be so loud. Now he understood why his parents had chosen such a distant planet to send him to: there was no doubt that they wanted him to start appreciating his familial links instead of using them to satisfy his curiosity.

People tended to take things for granted and value them more after losing them.

Being alone in his head was so unsettling. When Adam was with him, it was so much better.

Sighing, Harry flopped onto his stomach. He was terrible at not thinking about Adam. Maybe he should make more friends. The problem was, it turned out Harry wasn't very good at making human friends. Humans seemed to like him, but they also seemed to find him too odd and socially inept. Harry often either didn't get human jokes or laughed at inappropriate times, offending the other person. Only Adam seemed to find his social awkwardness endearing rather than offending.

"That's a whole minute I didn't think about Adam," Harry said with another sigh. He really was terribly clingy, wasn't he?

A sudden burst of music startled him. It took Harry a moment to realize it was his mobile phone. Harry reached out and grabbed it from the coffee table.

"Hey," Harry said, beaming into the darkness. He didn't need to see Caller's ID; there was only one person it could be.

"Hey, babe," Adam said. His voice sounded a little strange. "How are you doing?"

"Lots better now that you called," Harry said.

Adam chuckled softly. "God, you really don't have a coy bone in your body, do you?"

Harry furrowed his brows. He didn't understand why his tendency to tell what he thought was so unusual. He believed communication was key in all relationships.

"You keep saying it like it's a bad thing," Harry said.

"Not bad at all." Did Adam sound fond? "You're a dying breed, Haz."

His words were a little slurred.

Harry scrunched up his nose. "Are you drunk?"

"Just a little tipsy," Adam admitted.

"Aren't you on a date?" Harry said. He was hardly an expert on dating, but even he knew it wasn't appropriate to get drunk on a date.

"I'm just tipsy," Adam insisted. Harry wasn't sure he believed him. Adam's voice had never sounded like that: slow and ponderous.

"Anyway, he's boring," Adam said. "He talks boring. He looks boring. His eyes are boring, too."

Harry bit his lip to keep himself from laughing. Adam's slurred, drawling speech was so funny!

"Are you still on a date?"

"Yeah, but I'm in a restroom now," Adam said. "Wanted to call you, hear your voice. Anyone told you your voice is like a melody?"

Harry smiled. He had known his voice sounded melodic to human ears—Calluvian vocal cords were different. "Yes, but that's still really sweet of you to say."

Adam laughed, the sound a little hollow. "Sweet? Not really. You're the sweet one. So sweet I could eat you."

Harry's broke into giggles. "You really are drunk, not tipsy."

"Nah," Adam said. "I would say far worse stuff if I were drunk."

"Don't you have to return to your date?" Harry said. Not that he wanted Adam to, but after his conversation with Samantha he was determined to be a better friend.

"I guess I should," Adam said. He didn't sound all that excited by the prospect.

"Wanna come to my place?" Harry blurted out before he could stop himself.

It was official: he was a horrible friend. "We can watch a movie together." And cuddle.

There was silence on the line.

Then Adam said, "Fuck it. I'll be there in half an hour."

Harry grinned.

When the doorbell rang half an hour later, Harry opened the door and hugged Adam tightly. He couldn't help it. Despite his resolve not to be clingy, he felt...needy. He couldn't explain or rationalize it.

"How was your date?" he said belatedly. "Was it really that bad?"

Adam sighed, his breath brushing against Harry's cheek. "I don't want to talk about it," he said. His voice was no longer as slurred as it had been on the phone—the fresh air must have helped—but it was obvious he wasn't entirely sober.

Harry considered arguing before he realized he didn't really want to talk about Adam's date, either. "Samantha lent me the original series of Star Trek," Harry said instead, linking their hands and pulling Adam to the couch. "We should watch it! The special effects are hilarious!"

They did. They fell asleep on the couch during the third episode.

When Harry opened his eyes the next morning, he was greeted by the sight of Adam's sleeping face. They must have moved in their sleep, because Harry was sprawled on top of Adam now, their faces inches apart.

A sudden desire to do *something* confused Harry.

He didn't understand what exactly he wanted. He just knew that he liked looking at Adam—and that it wasn't enough.

Hesitantly, Harry lifted his hand and stroked Adam's chiseled jaw. The dark stubble scratched his palm. It felt strange. Not bad, though. A sudden image flashed in his mind: Adam's stubble scratching the sensitive skin of Harry's belly. Harry's stomach clenched.

"Haz?"

Harry snapped his eyes upward and smiled faintly when he saw that Adam was watching him with sleepy, heavy-lidded eyes. He was lucky Adam wasn't a telepath and couldn't know what a weird thought Harry had just had.

"Get off me, Haz," Adam said, his voice rough.

Frowning, Harry rolled off him and looked at him with concern. "Are you hungover? Does your head feel like splitting?" That was how a hangover was described in the book Harry had read a few days ago.

"No," Adam said, closing his eyes. Despite his words, he sounded pained. "Just give me a minute."

Shaking his head, Harry headed to the bathroom, bewildered.

He'd never understand humans.

Chapter 4

"I hate this place," Adam said two weeks later.

Harry, who was opening the pizza they had ordered, looked up.

Adam licked his lips. He wondered when he would finally stop feeling like kissing every inch of Harry's porcelain skin whenever Harry looked at him. That day couldn't come fast enough.

"You hate my flat?" Harry said.

Adam met his wounded gaze steadily, refusing to be moved by it. Although he knew Harry was oddly fond of this place, he wasn't going to keep pretending it was nice just to keep Harry happy.

"Don't you think it's claustrophobic, Haz?" Adam said. "It's tiny, dark, and too humid. I really hate leaving you here when I go home."

His lips pursed, Harry looked around the tiny room. "This is all I can afford."

Adam frowned. That couldn't be true.

He gave Harry ridiculously big tips in the hope that Harry would use the money to get a better place. "What do you do with the tips you get?"

"There's a blind homeless man who sits around the corner from the coffee shop," Harry said. "He needs that money more than me."

Looking at Harry's earnest face, Adam didn't have the heart to tell him that the man wasn't blind at all.

Adam pinched the bridge of his nose. It wasn't Harry's fault he thought the best of everyone. He wasn't angry at Harry. He was angry at the asshole who used Harry's kindness to scam him.

"Haz," he said. "Would you like to live with me? I have a spare room. And I'll drive you to work so you won't have to use the tube."

Harry stared at him. "Really?"

Adam smiled at Harry, trying to ignore the voice in the back of his head that kept saying he was making a huge mistake. "Really."

"Only if you let me pay you for the room," Harry said.

"Sure."

A small smile appeared on Harry's face before turning into a blinding one. "Thank you," he said before suddenly lunging forward and hugging Adam. "You're my favorite person," he said softly against Adam's neck.

Adam's throat tightened. He told himself not to read too much into it.

"You're mine, too."

He wasn't sure when it had happened, when this odd, ridiculous boy had crawled his way into his heart and settled there.

Fuck, sometimes he couldn't believe it had been just six weeks since he'd met Harry. Before Harry, Adam had always thought it was such a cliché when people said that it felt like they knew someone forever.

"I'm so glad my parents sent me here," Harry murmured, brushing his lips against Adam's throat. "You're my best friend."

Right.

"Yeah," Adam said, staring at the wall behind Harry. Right.

Chapter 5

Harry was a terrible flatmate.

He was messy, he was terrible at doing laundry, he put his feet on the coffee table, he left his things all over the flat, and he monopolized the TV to watch Discovery Channel.

Harry also fancied himself something of an interior decorator. He got weird little things at a garage sale and decorated the flat, claiming that the place lacked character.

One day Adam came home to see a giant painting in the living room that depicted something that vaguely resembled someone's puke.

"What is this, Hazza?" Adam said, torn between laughing and kissing him.

Harry beamed at him. "It's art, silly. Isn't it wonderful? The artist sold it to me for a mere ten pounds!"

Sometimes Adam was almost certain Harry was taking the piss, but looking into Harry's sincere, open expression, he knew he wasn't. Christ, Adam hadn't known it was possible to adore such a ridiculous person.

The day Harry discovered yoga was the worst. He asked Adam to go with him to buy a yoga mat and then couldn't make up his mind between a "sensible" brown one and a "cheerful" pink one. In the end, he bought the brown one and Adam bought him the pink one. After getting the yoga mats, Harry watched video tutorials and apparently decided he absolutely had to do yoga every evening wearing nothing but a pair of tiny white shorts that left nothing to the imagination.

Adam hated him. He hated Harry's legs, and his oddly-shaped knees, and his ridiculous white shorts.

Except he really, really didn't.

"You're a masochist, mate," Jake told him one day, a month after Harry had moved in with him.

He and Jake were lounging in front of Adam's TV, watching a Champion's League match. Harry, who didn't understand the point of football, was in the kitchen, humming some song and cooking, which was his latest obsession. Harry was pretty good at it, actually, even though everything he cooked was a bit too spicy.

Adam said, "We're just friends. Leave it."

He ignored the look of pity on Jake's face and focused his attention on the match.

Harry stuck his head out of the kitchen. "Anyone want ice cream? I made ice cream!"

"Sure, love," Adam said.

"What kind?" Jake asked, shooting Adam a look that he ignored.

"Lemon," Harry replied.

"Hmm, no thanks," Jake said. When Harry disappeared back into the kitchen, Jake looked at Adam. "Since when do you like lemon ice cream?"

"Shut it," Adam said without much heat.

Harry returned with a bowl of ice cream and a spoon. He gave them to Adam and snuggled up against him. "Who's winning?" he said without much interest, slinging an arm around Adam's middle.

"Barcelona," Adam said, ignoring Jake's stare, and dug into the ice cream. He brought the spoon to his mouth, swallowed, and suppressed a grimace. He really wasn't a fan of lemons.

"You don't like it," Harry said, his face falling.

"No, it's good," Adam said. "I just don't like lemons all that much."

The corners of Harry's mouth turned down. "Why didn't you just say so?" Harry murmured. "What's the point of my learning to cook if you don't like it?"

Adam stared at him. "You're learning to cook for me?"

"Of course," Harry said, looking at Adam like he was stupid. "You said you liked home-cooked food, and I wanted..." He averted his gaze, chewing on his lip. "You do so much for me. I wanted to give something back."

His chest tight with affection, Adam pecked him on the nose. "You don't have to, love."

"But I like it," Harry said quietly. He was still not meeting Adam's eyes, a slight blush on his cheeks. "I like doing things for you. It makes me feel good."

Adam suddenly wondered if it was the reason Harry insisted on doing his laundry, despite being rather terrible at it.

"Okay," Adam said, tucking the stray strand of Harry's hair behind his ear. Harry's hair had always fascinated him.

It was so soft and shiny it felt inhuman, like the finest silk. The hair wasn't the only thing about Harry that seemed ethereal: his skin was unnaturally flawless and soft to the touch, his eyes unnaturally violet and deep. Adam had to constantly stop himself from touching and stroking him all over.

"You need a haircut, babe," Adam said, running his fingers through Harry's hair. He tried not to stare at Harry's small pink mouth.

Harry closed his eyes, leaning into the touch. "I've been thinking of growing it out. What do you think?"

"It's your hair, Haz," Adam said, raising his eyebrows a little.

Lately, Harry had been asking for his opinion on his appearance all the time. Adam wasn't sure what to think of it. If he didn't know better, he'd think Harry wanted to look good for him, which…

It was a good thing he knew better. Friends. They were just friends.

"I know it's my hair," Harry said, rolling his eyes with a smile. "But do you think I'd look nice with long hair? I tried to grow it out once when I was, like, twelve or thirteen, because I wanted to be like my older brother, but I just looked ridiculous. But now I actually have cheekbones, so maybe I can pull it off now? What do you think?"

Adam brushed his thumb over said cheekbones. "You'd look good," he said, removing his hand when he noticed that Jake was watching them. "But you look good now, too."

An hour later, as he followed Jake to the door, Adam said, "Don't."

Jake looked at him grimly.

"Just be careful, man. He seems like a genuinely nice bloke, but the nice ones are usually the worst. You don't notice when they stab you in the gut because you're too distracted by their nice smiles."

Adam said nothing. He had a feeling it was too late for him anyway.

"Jake doesn't like me, does he?" Harry said when Adam returned to the living room.

Adam sighed inwardly. It had been probably too much to hope that Harry wouldn't notice. Harry could be very perceptive for someone who was completely oblivious to certain things.

"He's just a bit jealous," he lied, sitting down next to Harry. "He used to be my closest friend. We used to hang out all the time."

Harry looked down, an unhappy wrinkle appearing between his brows.

"It's not your fault," Adam said, slinging an arm around Harry and squeezing his shoulder.

"But it is," Harry said. "I do take a lot of your attention and time." Harry lifted his gaze. "You know the horrible part?" he said, his cheeks pink. "I'm not really sorry. I feel terrible because I don't feel sorry about it. I like having all of your attention. You're mine, not his."

Don't read too much into it.

Adam cleared his throat. "I can be both. Yours and his. It's not mutually exclusive. It's normal to have a few close friends."

Harry pursed his lips. "You don't call him babe."

Adam blinked. "No?" What did that have to do with anything?

A little wrinkle appeared between Harry's brows. "As long as I'm your only babe, he can be your friend, too, I guess."

Adam gave a snort. "Thanks for your permission, you little tyrant."

Harry laughed, having the grace to look embarrassed. "Sorry, I'm being awful. I don't know why I'm being so awful about it. Jake is very nice, but..." He wrapped his arm around Adam's middle and hid his face against his chest. "I never had a friend like you," he confessed quietly. "I have many friends back home, but this is different. You're different. I..." He lifted his head to look Adam in the eye. "I'm so happy that I met you. You make me very happy, all warm and giddy on the inside."

Adam told himself it was the language barrier. Harry simply had trouble expressing himself and didn't understand how his words sounded.

"I'm glad our friendship makes you happy," Adam said, kissing Harry on the temple. "I get what you mean: it's rare to find a person you fit so well with."

Harry nodded. "Thank you," he said, tugging at Adam's t-shirt. "For putting up with my weirdness," he clarified with a sheepish smile, tugging at Adam's t-shirt again.

"What are you doing?" Adam said. "Is my t-shirt offending you or something?"

"I like when you wear dress shirts and button-downs—I can just unbutton the top buttons and put my face there and smell you."

Adam stared at him. Of course he had noticed Harry's habit of undoing the top button of his shirt when they hugged, but he'd always thought it was just one of Harry's weird quirks.

Harry scrunched his nose up and laughed. "Did I say something weird again? I said something weird, didn't I?"

Christ, he was so fucking cute. Adam both hated and loved Harry's total lack of filter.

"You like how I smell?" he said, his voice huskier than he would have liked.

Harry nodded, frowning a little. "At first I thought it was your cologne. I tried it, but it doesn't smell the same. It's your skin. Smells really, really good." He looked at Adam's t-shirt with frustration before sighing and putting his head on Adam's shoulder with a pout.

It would have been adorable if Adam wasn't busy trying to control his body. He didn't want to imagine Harry rubbing his face against his bare chest, nuzzling into him like a kitten, then kissing his skin, licking his nipples—

Adam closed his eyes, trying to think of the most disgusting, hideous things to suppress his arousal.

"Harry," he said.

"Mmm?" Harry said, pressing his nose against the side of Adam's neck.

Adam gritted his teeth as Harry's lips rubbed against his skin. His cock started hardening, despite his best efforts not to react.

"Haz, enough," he managed, staring at the hideous painting on the wall.

"But why?"

"Because I'm only human."

Harry lifted his head, looking at him in bemusement. And fuck, Adam couldn't do it anymore.

"I'm gay, Harry," he said, pushing Harry away and getting to his feet.

"Don't you fucking get it? I'm gay. You're an attractive guy."

Harry stared at him, blinking, looking lost.

Fucking hell.

How could Haz be so naive? Was the possibility of Adam wanting him so far-fetched that it hadn't even occurred to him? It had never been more obvious that Harry simply didn't even see him as a sexual being. And damn, was it a blow to his ego...Adam was willing to admit he had always been a bit cocky. Not to sound conceited, but he knew how he looked. He'd never had trouble getting anyone he wanted—except for this weird, ridiculous, charming boy he had actual feelings for. Adam was pretty sure there was irony in this, somewhere.

"I..." Harry said, his eyes wide. "You can't—You know I don't—You know I can't—It's not because you—"

Adam chuckled. "It's not me, it's you? Don't bother, Haz. I get it." He turned away and went to his room.

Half an hour later, there was a tentative knock on the door.

"Go away, Harry," Adam said, without opening his eyes. Jake was right. He should put some distance between him and Harry, draw some healthy boundaries.

"Adam, please," Harry said.

He sounded sad—

No, damn you. Healthy boundaries.

"Can I come in?" Harry said. His voice cracked. "Please."

Fuck.

Adam got off the bed and went to the door. He didn't open it, though, because he knew one look at Harry's upset face would destroy his resolve.

"Harry, go to bed," he said. "We'll talk tomorrow when we are both calmer."

"I'm calm," Harry claimed, sounding anything but.

"You're not," Adam said.

"Okay, I'm not, but I won't be calmer if I have to wait until morning to talk to you."

Adam sighed and slid down to sit on the floor, his back to the door. "All right, talk. Make it short, though."

"Like this? Through the door?"

"Yes," Adam said succinctly. Harry didn't need to know how much power his face had over him. He had some pride left.

He heard Harry sit down on the other side of the door.

For a long moment, there was only silence.

"I'm sorry," Harry said at last. "I'm sorry for being an idiot and not realizing how uncomfortable I was making you."

Adam frowned. That wasn't what he expected.

"I'm just," Harry said. "I've been kind of sheltered all my life. I have never been so close to... unmarried sexually active people much. So it had never been an issue before, you know? That's why it hadn't occurred to me that you could be... attracted to me." There was still a note of bemusement in Harry's voice, as if he couldn't completely believe it.

Despite himself, Adam smiled. Harry was so odd. Hadn't he seen himself in the mirror? Sometimes he really was like an alien, because his standards seemed so different from normal.

Adam pinched the bridge of his nose.

"It's not your fault, Haz," he said with a sigh. "This is my problem, and I already know how to deal with it."

"How?" Harry said.

"There will be rules. We'll both follow them."

"What sort of rules?"

"We'll be friends like Jake and I are friends."

He could almost hear Harry frown. It was a little disturbing how vividly he could imagine it.

"But—but," Harry stammered, sounding positively crushed.

"Harry," Adam said, closing his eyes. "Please don't make it harder."

Harry was silent for a long time.

At last, he said, sounding absolutely deflated, "Okay. If that's what you want." Adam heard him get up and go to his own bedroom, the door shutting quietly after him.

"Want," Adam repeated before laughing, the sound harsh and ugly in the silence of the room. No, that wasn't what he wanted. But it hardly mattered.

Chapter 6

"Adam is attracted to me," Harry said.

Samantha stopped wiping the counter and lifted her head. "And?"

Harry frowned, not understanding why she wasn't surprised. "That's it. Adam is attracted to me."

She raised her eyebrows. "Is that supposed to be news to me? Why do you think I've been calling him your boyfriend? He looks at you like you're his personal sun."

Harry's frown deepened. She was wrong. Adam didn't look at him that way. He felt like Adam barely looked at him lately.

Harry shook his head. "As I understand it, it's just physical attraction. He's gay and he considers me physically attractive."

Not that he understood the concept of physical attraction all that well. At times like this, Harry felt more acutely than ever that he didn't belong to this world.

Samantha rolled her eyes. "Sure, and I'm the Queen. What's the problem, Hazza? The guy's insanely attractive and hot, well off, nice, not without sense of humor, and he adores you. I'm practically green with envy." She smirked. "I bet he's great in bed. He looks like he's great in bed."

Rubbing behind his neck, Harry chuckled. "Don't be ridiculous. Adam is my friend, not a..." He blushed at the thought of physical intimacy outside a marriage bond. Humans' casual attitude toward sex still baffled him a little. When he had found out that humans could have sex as early as twelve, he had been absolutely flabbergasted. Back home most people didn't have sex before their bonding ceremony at the age of twenty-five. Sex outside of a bond was such a taboo back home that he felt embarrassed even thinking about it. It wasn't that Calluvians were prudish about sex. It was just...until the bonding ceremony, Calluvians weren't supposed to be interested in sex.

There were rumors that sometimes, when the childhood bond was weak, it was possible to feel sexual attraction to someone other than one's bondmate, but Harry wasn't sure how truthful those rumors were. His own childhood bond had always been perfectly strong and he'd never felt even a flicker of sexual attraction toward anyone. It had never bothered him. He'd had no reason to feel bothered about something he was incapable of feeling—yet.

But now he was curious. He wanted to understand Adam. For the first time ever, Harry wondered if he was missing something because of the bond.

It had been over four thousand years since Calluvians had started practicing childhood bonds. The practice had been put in place for a reason.

It all had started when a minor member of the First Grand Clan kidnapped the queen of the Third Grand Clan and forced an archaic, unbreakable bond on her. Although there had been precedents of forced bonds in the past, no one had ever tried to force an unbreakable bond on the ruler of a grand clan. The uproar had been enormous. That type of bond had become obsolete for a reason—it was impossible to dissolve—so a mind rapist effectively became a royal consort despite best mind adepts' efforts to break the bond.

Eventually, the queen had to step down in favor of her brother. To make matters worse, the First Grand Clan refused to be held responsible for its member's harmful actions against the Third Royal House, even though it was legally obligated to do so.

As a result, the political scandal turned into a military conflict, eventually involving all of the grand clans in the greatest planet-wide war in the Calluvian history that nearly wiped out the entire population when the biological weapons used in the war affected the population's health and reproductive ability.

The Great War ended years later when everyone realized how close to extinction they had come. It took decades to recover from that devastating war and its consequences.

To prevent something like that from happening again, the Council of the Grand Clans had come up with the way to bond children's telepathic cores from early age. A childhood bond worked differently from any other telepathic bond, digging itself deep into the child's psyche and making it impossible for someone to force a marriage bond.

Any other time such a proposal would have likely led to a debate on consent issues, since children couldn't give their consent, but after years of bloodshed and decades of rebuilding, no one wanted something like that to happen again and pretty much everyone had just been relieved by the solution.

Well, not everyone. Some people had refused to follow the law and left their grand clans, but it wasn't appropriate to acknowledge their existence in polite company. *Renegades*, they were called in whispers. *Rebels.* Those people didn't acknowledge any grand clan's authority. They were effectively wanted outlaws, but no one knew where they lived. Some said that they lived somewhere high up in the Great Mountains, but Harry didn't think it was true. Wouldn't modern technology find them if that were the case?

Anyway, the rebels were the only people on Calluvia who didn't have childhood bonds. Harry had always thought that the rebels were wrong. The fact that there hadn't been any conflicts like that again proved that the Bonding Law was right. It had been scientifically proven that bonding children's telepathic cores made their telepathy more stable and their tempers milder. Sociologists insisted that childhood bonds had basically saved their society from self-destruction—something that happened to too many advanced civilizations.

But how could he explain it to Samantha? Especially since Harry didn't fully understand how the bond worked. There was very little information on the bond in the public database. Why did the bond prevent people from feeling attraction?

Why were some bonded people capable of feeling some sexual attraction while others couldn't feel a thing until the bonding ceremony? What happened during the bonding ceremony? How did a childhood bond become a marriage bond? Harry had asked his brother once, but Ksar had said that Harry didn't really want to know. When Harry had asked his mother, she had just given him an odd look and changed the subject. It was so weird. Why were they so tight-lipped about it? What were they hiding? Why?

"I'm engaged, remember?" Harry said, for lack of anything better to say.

"Please," Samantha said with a scoff. "In all the time you've worked here, she's never called you, Harry. What kind of relationship is that?"

Harry winced. He hated that he couldn't defend Leylen'shni'gul. But revealing that he wasn't human and effectively making an unauthorized Contact with Terrans would be a violation of one of the most important intergalactic laws. Even if Harry didn't get arrested for that, he had no doubt the scandal would be used as a weapon by his mother's political enemies. If his mother didn't kill him for putting her in such a weak position, Harry's brother would.

"It's not Leyla's fault that she's unable to keep in touch," Harry said.

It was true.

Lately he could barely feel the bond between them. Their telepathic connection had disappeared immediately upon his arrival on Earth, but he had still been able to feel their bond at the back of his mind, like a constant reassuring presence.

However, as the time passed, the bond had gradually weakened, and Harry was afraid it would fade completely soon, just like his links to his family had upon his arrival. Granted, he had never heard of a childhood bond fading completely. It was pretty common for weaker telepathic connections to fade if the physical distance was too big to maintain them, but the childhood bond was too strong for that. As far as Harry knew, it never happened.

And yet, his mind was so very quiet lately, for the first time in his life. Coupled with the distance between him and Adam, this was the most depressed Harry had ever felt.

Harry sighed at the thought of Adam.

"I don't buy it," Samantha said.

It took Harry a moment to remember what they were talking about. Right. His bondmate's "neglect" of him.

"It doesn't bother me," Harry said with a shake of his head. Why couldn't Samantha concentrate on the real issue? "Adam is attracted to me. What should I do?"

She gave him a look. "What do you mean? If you don't want him, just tell him so, and move out of his place."

"No," Harry said, his brows drawing together. He didn't want to move out. He loved living with Adam, and he wanted to live with him for as long as he could—while he still could. His parents might recall him any day now.

His stomach knotted at the thought. He missed his family terribly, but the thought of leaving Adam made him feel ill and panicky.

Noticing the odd expression on Samantha's face, Harry said, "What?"

"Harry, you do understand that it must be... uncomfortable for him, right? Unreciprocated attraction is no joke. It must be hard for him to live with you."

"I…" Harry swallowed. "I do. That's why I'm asking advice. I don't want to hurt him."

Samantha sighed. "I don't know what to say. That's a tough situation. Are you sure you aren't attracted to him at all? When I see you with him, his attraction to you doesn't really look unrequited."

Harry chuckled. "Don't be silly!"

"Silly?" she said, her voice full of exasperation. "Haz, you show the classic signs of attraction: you angle your body toward him, you smile looking him in the eye, you are constantly all over him, you find the lamest excuses to touch him. Just a few days ago, I saw you nuzzling his neck and you looked like you were getting off on it! Frankly, the fact that you are *not* attracted to him is more surprising to me. Are you sure you aren't?"

"I'm—I'm," Harry stammered, his mind racing. "I think so?"

She stared at him. "How can you not know?"

Harry wondered what she would say if he told her he was an alien with a completely different biological makeup. At this point it would probably be more believable than his obliviousness and inexperience.

"I'm something you would probably call demisexual," he said carefully. "I'm closer to asexual. I don't really get attraction. I have to be… emotionally connected to the person to feel any sexual attraction." He needed to be telepathically bonded, which he obviously wasn't—not to Adam, at least.

Samantha had a pinched expression on her face. "Harry," she said slowly. "Are you saying you don't feel emotionally connected to Adam? Because that's the biggest pile of bullshit I've ever heard."

Harry looked at her, feeling completely lost.

"Can you describe what attraction feels like?" he said haltingly, licking his lips. "It's probably a stupid question, but humor me?"

Samantha smiled at him. "It's not a stupid question if you identify as demisexual or asexual." She looked thoughtful. "Well, I'm not a man, but when I'm attracted to someone, I feel excited around them, want to touch them all the time, I smile around them more, want to please them, want to look good for them, want them to think I'm funny and interesting. Obviously there are physical signs..."

"What physical signs?"

She stared at him. "You really want to know what I feel when I'm turned on?"

Harry fought a blush. This was so incredibly embarrassing. But he needed to know—because everything else she had described sounded very familiar. Confusingly familiar.

Biting his lip, Harry nodded. He wasn't a baby. He could talk about sex. It wasn't a big deal for humans and he was supposed to be a human.

"Okay." Samantha blushed. "My skin tingles when he touches me. I get a warm feeling in my lower stomach. I want his hands on my body. I want to be close to him so there's no space between us. I want his lips on me, everywhere." She was red now. "I get wet if I'm really attracted to the guy, but obviously it's different for men. Men get hard." She smiled a little. "I didn't expect to have this talk until I have teenage kids."

Harry didn't smile back. While some of the things she had said didn't apply to him, some things were more than a little familiar.

He always wanted to be close to Adam, press his body flush against him. He wanted Adam's hands on his body all the time. He had never imagined Adam's mouth on his body, but now that he did, the thought wasn't…unpleasant. It made his heart beat faster and his skin warm.

But he didn't entirely understand what getting wet or hard had to do with being attracted to someone. Well, he understood the mechanics of sex, but having never experienced it, it was difficult to imagine.

"I guess you would call my parents… prudish," Harry said, choosing his words carefully. He knew his obliviousness must seem strange in the era of Google. "They disapprove of sex out of wedlock. They never talked to me about sex and discouraged me from learning about it."

Samantha's eyes widened. "Really?"

Harry nodded, feeling a pang of guilt for lying. His parents weren't really that prudish. Calluvians simply didn't discuss sex unless it was necessary.

"…Harry?"

Flinching, Harry looked back at Samantha. "Sorry, what?"

She shook her head. "I don't get something. If you've never been attracted to anyone, how can you be engaged to that girl?" She scoffed. "Please don't tell me it's an arranged marriage. But after what you said about your parents, that wouldn't surprise me."

"It is an arranged marriage," Harry conceded, though he'd never thought of his childhood bond in those terms. "But I do like my fiancée. She's nice."

"Honestly," Samantha said. "Where are you from again? Fifteenth century? It's positively medieval."

Harry chuckled, wondering what she would say if she knew that Harry's people were actually thousands of years ahead of humans technologically. But it was rather curious that his people's customs were closer to the customs that humans had practiced several centuries ago.

"So are you attracted to Adam or not?" Samantha said.

Harry averted his gaze. The answer that should have been simple was anything but. He did have some strange feelings toward Adam that he had never felt before. He did feel weirdly drawn to Adam. But was it attraction?

No, he was probably just confused. He got neither "wet" nor "hard" around Adam. That had to mean he wasn't attracted to him, right?

"No," Harry replied. "I don't think I'm attracted to him." He rubbed his nose with a sigh. "I need to figure out what to do. I don't like Adam's solution."

"Adam's solution?"

Harry felt the corners of his mouth turn down. "He's been different the past few days."

"Different?"

"He's, like, friendly, but he's distant." Harry caught his bottom lip between his teeth and looked down at his hands. He said quietly, "He hasn't called me 'babe' or 'love' in two days."

Silence.

"Let me get this straight, Haz," Samantha said, her tone very dry. "You want him to call you love and baby, and you're upset that he doesn't anymore."

"Babe," Harry corrected, frowning. "Not baby."

She gave him a strange look before giving a laugh. "God, you're so weird, Harry." But then, she became serious. "You want my advice? Figure out what you feel for him before it's too late. Maybe it's just me, but I don't get upset because my best friend doesn't use endearments on me."

Harry opened his mouth and closed it.

She was right. It shouldn't have upset him. No one in his family called him such things and Harry didn't doubt his family's love. But it was different with Adam. He loved being Adam's love and Adam's babe. He *wanted* Adam to call him love and babe, which was…probably a weird thing to want from one's friend.

Harry buried his face in his hands, groaning in a mix of embarrassment and frustration. "I don't understand anything anymore."

Samantha just laughed.

Chapter 7

Samantha's words were still on his mind as Harry got into Adam's car after the end of his shift.

"Hey," Adam said with a neutral smile. He looked tired and less immaculate than usual, his stubble so thick it could almost be called a beard. It would probably be rough to the touch.

Harry looked away, curling his fingers in his lap and resisting the urge to kiss Adam on the cheek. The longer he went without physical contact with Adam, the harder it became to suppress impulses like that.

"Hi!" Harry said, trying to sound cheerful. For Adam's sake, he had been trying to act like the distance between them didn't bother him. Harry hoped he was convincing, but he wasn't sure.

"How was your day?" Adam said, pulling out of the parking lot.

Harry tried not to frown. It should have been "How was your day, love?" with Adam running his fingers through Harry's hair or stroking his nape as Harry curled into him.

"Good," Harry replied, rubbing his palms over his thighs. He hated that he couldn't touch Adam. If Adam's friendship with Jake was like that, no wonder Jake had been jealous. "How was yours?"

Adam hummed something noncommittal, his eyes on the traffic.

A slightly awkward silence settled between them for the rest of the drive. Harry hated every second of it.

"Can we talk?" Harry said when they arrived home.

Adam shrugged his jacket off and lifted his head. "What?" he said. His face gave nothing away.

Do you hate me now?

Harry opened his mouth, but nothing came out. He lost his nerve. He couldn't ask it. He was afraid to ask. It was always at the back of his mind that he didn't even need to ask if he truly wanted to know. He could find out easily enough. He'd never been more scared to use his telepathy in his life.

Harry wet his lips. "Do you want me to move out?" he said haltingly. "I can move out if that's what you want."

Adam shook his head stiffly, his shoulders tense as he unbuttoned the top buttons of his shirt without looking at Harry. "Don't be silly, Haz."

Harry stared at Adam's half-bare chest. He wished he could bury his face there, breathe in Adam's scent and stay like that forever.

A strong, unfamiliar feeling washed over him. It felt a little like dizziness but was almost pleasant.

Perhaps he had caught some alien bug? Although he had received all the proper shots before leaving his planet, there was always a small chance. He should probably go lie down. Just in case.

Harry muttered that he wasn't hungry and headed to his room. His stomach dropped when Adam didn't even try to stop him. Maybe he really should move out.

It was his last thought as Harry fell into a strange, exhausted sleep as soon as his head touched the pillow.

He dreamed of silence, something stretching and breaking with a snap. Suddenly, he was burning from the inside out, feeling thirsty and hungry and oversensitive—

Harry woke up with a start, his breathing heavy and unsteady, his heart racing with agitation.

He sat up, unsure what he'd been dreaming about. He breathed in and out, trying to calm down.

But he couldn't.

There was something wrong. There was something wrong with him. He felt off, unstable, his control over his telepathy shattered to pieces. He could feel faint echoes of other people's thoughts. One floor down, a woman was angry at her husband for watching football and not paying her attention, and her husband was wondering when she would fall asleep so that he could sneak out to meet another woman.

Harry took a deep breath, trying to take control of his telepathy. He supposed he should be grateful that it was night and there weren't many people awake. Sleeping people didn't give off clear thoughts, just a background buzz he could ignore more easily.

Harry pressed his hands to his temples and closed his eyes, concentrating on rebuilding his mental shields.

He went rigid when he realized that something was wrong *in* his mind. Something was missing. His bond. His bond to Leylen'shni'gul was gone, every faint remnant of it.

But that wasn't all. His senses had never been so strong. He could hear better. He could hear even Adam's steady breaths in the other room.

Adam.

A longing hit him so strongly Harry shuddered. He had to get to Adam. He needed Adam.

Harry rolled out of the bed and stumbled out of his room. He stopped a few times, taken aback by how acutely and vividly he could feel the cold floor under his bare feet. Everything seemed more vivid: the sensations, the smells, the sounds—the strange hunger inside him.

Shivering, Harry pushed Adam's door open and walked to his bed. It should have been impossible to see so clearly in the dark, but, to Harry's confusion, he could see pretty well.

Adam was sleeping on his back, his long, muscular chest rising and falling steadily.

He was half-naked.

Harry wasn't sure why he was so fixated on that fact, but suddenly that was all he could think about as he stared at Adam. He needed—he needed something. He wanted something. He wanted to get naked, climb into Adam's bed and rub his bare skin against Adam's.

Harry swallowed, confused and scandalized by his thoughts but unable to stop them. He felt a strange pleasant sort of dizziness again, and then a heavy ache in his lower body.

"Harry?"

Adam's sleepy, hoarse voice did weird things to him.

"Yeah, it's me," Harry managed. His own voice sounded odd, thick and breathless.

Adam sat up, squinting at him in the darkness. "What's wrong? What are you doing here?"

"I..." Harry said. "I needed to see you."

"In the middle of the night?" Adam said, reaching out to the bedside lamp. When the soft light illuminated the room, Adam kept his eyes on Harry's face, carefully avoiding looking at his body.

Harry breathed in and breathed out deeply, trying and failing to make sense of the changes in his body. At least he had managed to get control over his telepathy, but it was small comfort when his entire body seemed to be put wrong.

"I think... I think I'm sick," Harry croaked out. Maybe he had really caught some alien bug after all.

"What?" Adam was by his side immediately, his hand on Harry's forehead. "You're a little warm," he said, frowning. His long fingers stroked Harry's cheek.

Harry shivered, a strange sensation coursing through his body. The throbbing ache in his lower half intensified. Harry let out a small sound when Adam's finger brushed his ear.

"You're trembling," Adam said. His other hand cupped Harry's cheek.

Harry leaned into Adam's touch. He missed Adam's hands. He wanted Adam to touch him all the time.

"Babe?"

Harry whimpered, pressing his face into Adam's chest and nuzzling into it. Babe. He was Adam's babe. "Yeah," he murmured, wrapping his arms tightly around Adam. It felt so good, but the ache in his lower body actually increased, becoming nearly unbearable. "I need you."

"Fuck," Adam said. "Haz—you're hard."

Harry opened his eyes and blinked. What?

Looking down, Harry stared.

His underwear was tented. His cock was erect.

That wasn't all. His briefs felt a little sticky. Something—some sort of slick—was leaking out of his hole.

It... it had never happened to him before. Of course Harry knew what it meant, but it shouldn't have happened. It shouldn't have been possible.

But it was useless to deny it: this was sexual attraction. Arousal. His body wanted sex. His body wanted Adam. It should have been impossible. He wasn't bonded to Adam.

No, he wasn't bonded to *anyone*. He had forgotten about it. His bond was gone. With the bond broken, this was probably normal. Probably. He wasn't sure.

"Harry," Adam said roughly. His face was suddenly so close. His lips ghosted over the corner of Harry's mouth, just the faintest, briefest, most maddening brush of lips— and his breath was sharp and hot, and his hands were trembling a little as they fluttered across Harry's back, as if he wasn't sure. Harry let out a sound, a helpless, desperate, choking sort of plea, because he needed him closer—and Adam was suddenly there, his hips pressed against Harry's, and his body felt long and hard and perfect—right there.

Adam's breathing was ragged. "Go now if you don't want this." Adam's lips brushed against his earlobe, and Harry whined quietly, digging his nails into Adam's shoulder blades. He wanted Adam closer, tighter, he wanted more. He was struck by a sudden *need* to know what Adam's mouth would taste like.

Adam let out a pained, low sound and dragged his lips across Harry's jawline. His mouth was so close. "Are you sure, babe?"

Harry wasn't sure of anything, but he wanted this hungry ache to go away and he had a feeling only Adam could sate it.

He nodded dazedly, parting his lips just in time for Adam's tongue. He moaned, enjoying the taste of Adam's mouth, of his stubble scratching his chin. It felt so good. So very good. Adam's fingers buried themselves in Harry's hair, holding him still while Adam gave him one bruising kiss after another, kissing like he wanted to climb inside Harry and live there—and Harry wanted him to.

"Fuck, you're so sweet," Adam rasped out between the drugging kisses, tilting Harry's head the way he wanted with strong but gentle hands.

Harry melted into him, his thoughts muddled with foggy pleasure mixed with need. No matter how hard Adam kissed him, it didn't seem to relieve the needy ache in his lower body. If anything, it made it worse. He was aching terribly, *wanting*.

"I need," Harry mumbled against Adam's mouth, trying to kiss Adam harder. "Please."

"Yeah," Adam said, pushing Harry toward the bed.

Harry fell on the mattress gracelessly, making a frustrated noise when he lost physical contact with Adam. But before long, Adam was behind him, kissing his neck with parted lips, leaving wet trails, his large hands roaming all over Harry's chest, his quivering stomach—

Harry keened when Adam's hands kneaded his thighs. So close—

As if hearing his thoughts, Adam dragged his underwear off and wrapped a large hand around Harry's throbbing cock. Harry gasped, his mouth falling open as Adam started stroking his cock slowly. It felt so good but so frustrating, and before long, Harry was whining, squirming constantly and trying to relieve the ache inside him. He didn't understand what he needed, but this wasn't enough. He wanted—he wanted…

He wanted to stop feeling *empty*. He wanted the hard thing pressed against his ass—Adam's cock. Yes, that was what he wanted.

Harry reached back and grabbed it. It was thick, and long, and heavy in his hand. It felt perfect. He wanted it, wanted it inside, wanted it to fill him up.

He nudged it between his legs, but his aim was off, and Adam's cock rubbed against his inner thigh.

Adam sucked a breath in. "Haz…" he said into Harry's nape, grinding his cock against Harry's ass for a moment before pushing Harry's thighs together and feeding his leaking cock between them.

Harry gasped as Adam's cock rubbed against the sensitive skin of his inner thighs and grazed over his hole. This wasn't what he had wanted—he wanted Adam inside him—but his words died on his lips as Adam started thrusting, fucking his thighs.

Harry couldn't decide if he hated it or loved it. He moaned weakly every time Adam's cock grazed against his hole—so close, so good, not enough. He was nearly sobbing with frustration before Adam finally took Harry's cock back into his hand and started pumping it hard in time with his thrusts.

This was better, but it still wasn't enough.

He wanted to be filled up, he wanted the ache to go away, he wanted—

Adam's cock nudged hard against his hole, almost catching on the rim. Harry cried out, his mouth going slack as pleasure washed over his body. His cock softened in Adam's hand, the demanding throbbing in his hole finally lessening. He felt so good, like he was floating on a cloud.

"Good?" Adam said, his voice tight and barely recognizable. He turned Harry onto his back.

Harry nodded dreamily and watched through heavy-lidded eyes as Adam sat up, took his own cock into his hand and start pumping it hard and fast, his dark eyes roaming all over Harry's body.

"Can I come on you, Haz?" Adam ground out.

Harry nodded, although he wasn't entirely sure what exactly he was agreeing to. It didn't matter; at the moment he would let Adam do anything he wanted. He would always let Adam do anything he wanted.

He watched Adam clench his jaw, watched his magnificent body tense up and go rigid, before a low groan ripped out of Adam's throat and then Adam was coming, his ejaculate covering Harry's chest and thighs.

"So fucking beautiful," Adam muttered, sounding drunk and dazed as he looked at Harry's body underneath him. "So beautiful, the sweetest, the prettiest—fucking adore you."

Harry smiled, preening a little. Adam adored him. Adam thought he was beautiful and sweet.

"I adore you, too," Harry said sleepily as Adam cleaned his chest and thighs with some tissues.

He yawned and buried his face on Adam's chest when Adam finally stretched out next to him.

"Best birthday present ever," Adam murmured, stroking his fingers through Harry's hair.

It took a lot of effort for Harry to open his eyes. "Wait, today is your birthday?"

Adam smiled at him, kissed him on the nose, and nodded. "I'm officially twenty-seven as of two hours ago."

"You should have told me. I didn't get you a present."

"I don't need a better present," Adam said, stroking his nape.

Harry smiled at him sleepily. "I'm still making you a birthday dinner and we're celebrating at home after work."

"All right," Adam said. "Now sleep, love. We'll talk tomorrow."

Harry closed his eyes and let himself drift away, listening to the steady beat of Adam's heart. He would worry about his bond and the consequences of his actions tomorrow. Right now he felt too good to worry about anything. He was in Adam's arms, warm, safe, and cherished.

Nothing bad could happen.

Chapter 8

Harry woke up feeling good and happy. He sighed sleepily, burrowing deeper into his amazing-smelling pillow. His amazing pillow moved. Harry pouted and clung to it harder.

"Let go, Haz," Adam said with a chuckle, kissing him on the temple. "I have to go to work."

"Don't go," Harry murmured, nuzzling into Adam's chest. He smelled so good. "It's your birthday. You deserve a day off. I don't have a shift today. We can celebrate."

"I can't," Adam said, stroking Harry's cheek with his fingers. "We can celebrate in the evening. Now open your pretty eyes for me."

Harry forced his eyes open and rubbed at them. When his bleary gaze focused on Adam, his breath caught in his throat. Adam's dark eyes held so much affection and warmth it melted Harry's heart.

Then, he realized he was sprawled on Adam's chest. Adam's very naked chest. Adam's very naked everything.

Harry felt himself flush. Last night seemed so surreal now. Had it really happened?

"Hey," Adam said, his voice still deep and hoarse from sleep.

"Happy Birthday," Harry said, feeling a little shy and bewildered.

"Thanks, love," Adam said, gazing at him with hooded eyes. He looked so... good. Harry felt something tug low in his stomach, his lips tingling with the sudden urge to press them against Adam's jawline. His cock twitched.

"Don't look at me like that," Adam said with a soft chuckle. "I really have to go to work, babe."

Babe. Adam had called him love and babe again. Did that mean they were back to normal? Or had last night changed everything?

Harry rubbed his cheek against Adam's chest, unsure.

What happened last night... was it wrong? It didn't feel wrong.

But sex outside a marriage bond was considered wrong back home.

Technically, he wasn't bonded at the moment.

But he was still promised to Leylen'shni'gul. There was a marriage contract and everything.

It wasn't his fault the bond had dissolved.

Harry sighed, realizing he was arguing with himself like a madman.

"What's with that face?" Adam said, tipping Harry's face up to meet his eyes. His lips pressed together briefly. "Any regrets?"

Harry didn't feel regret. And that was the problem, wasn't it?

Shouldn't he feel guilty? Was what he'd done with Adam immoral? He wasn't sure. A childhood bond was different from the human concept of romantic engagement. Harry didn't feel like he'd betrayed Leylen'shni'gul. He hadn't given her any promises—his parents had done it for him years ago. Harry supposed now he could understand why renegades thought that bonding children when they couldn't give their consent was messed up.

Harry shook his head in response. "I don't regret it. It's just...you know about Leyla."

Adam's expression darkened. He opened his mouth but then glanced at the clock on the wall and rolled off the bed. "Fuck, I'm really late. We'll talk when I'm back, okay?"

Harry nodded. He watched Adam get ready for work. Within ten minutes, Adam was ready to go.

"Goodbye hug?" Harry said uncertainly. He wanted more than a goodbye hug, but he felt a bit embarrassed by the wanton thoughts that crossed his mind as he watched Adam dress. He didn't recognize himself, and it threw him off. Was he a different person without the bond? Did the bond change a person so much?

Instead of responding, Adam walked to the bed and pulled Harry to him.

Harry returned the embrace eagerly, his nipples tingling as they rubbed against the fabric of Adam's suit. He parted his lips, wanting a kiss.

"How am I supposed to leave this room?" Adam said, sighing into his cheek.

Harry turned his face, and their lips met in a needy, wet kiss that made Harry dizzy.

He'd always found it curious that so many civilizations shared the custom of romantic kissing with lips. Harry had kissed his bondmate once—he'd been curious and she was similarly curious—but they both had found the experience awkward and pointless. It had felt nothing like kissing Adam. Kissing Adam felt as natural and necessary as breathing. He didn't know how to stop.

By the time Adam stepped away, Harry's knees felt like jelly and he was painfully hard again.

"I'll be back soon," Adam said, his cheekbones flushed and his eyes almost black as he stared at Harry with exhilarating intensity. "As soon as I can."

As the door closed after Adam, Harry fell back on the mattress and stared unseeingly at the ceiling, feeling out of breath and hot all over his body.

What was this overwhelming feeling that made him want to run after Adam and glue them together? Harry wasn't sure he liked it. It was the most intense—and scariest— thing he'd ever felt.

* * *

Harry felt pretty pleased with himself.

The dinner was ready, the table was set, and the cake he'd worked so hard on for most of the afternoon looked delicious (it was a little crooked, but Harry hoped that it wasn't obvious). Hopefully it tasted delicious, too.

Harry looked at it anxiously, wondering not for the first time whether he should have just bought a birthday cake from the bakery around the corner. He did like the idea of baking a homemade cake for Adam, but what if it wasn't good? What if Adam hated it?

Well, it was too late anyway. Adam should be home soon.

Wiping his hands on his t-shirt, Harry glanced at the table for the last time, making sure everything was perfect—

He felt a familiar tickling sensation.

Frowning, Harry looked at his body and froze, his eyes widening.

A semi-transparent white force field was starting to surround his body, becoming denser with each second. Then, there was a familiar pulling sensation sweeping through him, and Harry barely managed to think, *No*, when he was yanked through space, the whites of the stars streaking by in a blur.

Humans were wrong in their assumption that aliens would arrive in spaceships. Aliens, at least aliens from Harry's corner of the galaxy, had all but stopped using spaceships thousands of years ago when that method of transportation had become obsolete with the invention of the transgalactic teleporter. Spaceships were now used only for short distances by touristic companies and by lower classes who couldn't afford the TNIT—Transgalactic Nearly Instantaneous Teleportation.

"Welcome home, Your Highness."

Harry gazed blankly at the familiar high ceilings and transparent walls giving the illusion of being outside.

He was home.

"Your Highness?"

If he was home, it meant he wouldn't find out if the cake he'd baked for Adam's birthday was any good.

"Your Highness?"

Adam, who was half a galaxy away.

Adam, who would come home to an empty flat.

Adam, whom he was unlikely to ever see again.

Harry swallowed, his throat clogging up and his chest growing tight.

"Your Highness!"

He flinched and looked around. Realizing that the voice belonged to the palace's AI, he felt silly—silly and strange. He'd gotten too used to being on Earth, to their charmingly outdated technology.

Harry cleared his throat, trying to get rid of the thick lump lodged there. "Yes?"

"Her Majesty and the King-Consort are waiting for you in Her Majesty's study."

"Thank you, Borg'gorn." Harry left the transporter room and headed for his mother's study, his feet heavy and his heart heavier.

He'd been away for months. He missed the palace, missed his parents, missed his siblings, but he couldn't quite muster up the excitement and happiness he was probably supposed to be feeling right now. He could feel his familial connections coming back to life in his mind, but now they seemed loud and intrusive instead of comforting.

Harry tightened his mental shields, surrounding his mind as best as he could. He was out of practice; he hadn't needed to protect his mind from telepaths on Earth.

Earth, which was thousands of light years away.

Forcing the thought out of his mind, Harry pushed

the door to his mother's study open.

His parents turned their heads.

Harry put on a smile and waited for them to acknowledge him first.

Zahef'ngh'chaali was the one to do it. "Harht," his father said, gazing at him with a warm smile. "Welcome home. You were missed."

Harry felt his father reach for him telepathically and lowered his mental shields, allowing his father's mind to embrace his. He sighed as the familiar warmth and comfort of his father's mind enveloped him. He'd missed this, but he found himself wishing for a physical hug, for strong arms holding him tightly—

His throat closed up again and Harry blinked rapidly, trying to get rid of the sudden moisture in his eyes.

"Harht'ngh'chaali, health and tranquility," his mother said, her voice a little sterner than his father's.

Queen Tamirs'shni'chaali had always been the stern parent, but Harry supposed that came with the job of being the Queen of the Second Grand Clan of Calluvia. Of course his mother was stern; she had to be when she was responsible for so many people.

It didn't mean she didn't love her children; Harry knew she did.

"Health and tranquility, Mother," he said, trying not to sound subdued. The traditional greeting seemed strange after humans' informal greetings.

His mother's brows furrowed when her mind touched his. "You're upset," she said. "Are you upset because you expected us to recall you home sooner?"

"Can I go back?" Harry blurted out.

When his parents stared at him, he added uncertainly, "Just for a little while? I was in the middle of something when I was transported home."

His parents exchanged a look, communicating telepathically through their bond. The bond he still didn't have in his mind. Was it broken irrevocably?

"Why do you want to return to Sol III?" his mother said at last.

"Terra," his father corrected his wife gently.

"Humans call it Earth now, actually," Harry said, desperately trying to think of a good reason. He was afraid "It's Adam birthday" wouldn't be accepted as a good enough reason. Long-distance teleportation to a planet half a galaxy away was very resource-consuming and expensive, even for the direct heirs of grand clans like Harry, but it wasn't the only reason people couldn't use it on a whim. Earth was a pre-TNIT planet; any visits to pre-TNIT planets were regulated by the Ministry of Intergalactic Affairs. Generally, only one trip a year was allowed per individual.

"Answer the question, Harht'ngh'chaali," his mother said.

He suddenly hated the sound of his own name. It sounded so pretentious. Unfortunately, the more highborn one was, the longer their name got. Harry liked human names so much better.

But he wasn't human. He seemed to have forgotten that.

"I'd like you to call me Harry," Harry said, looking down.

"Harry," his mother repeated flatly.

Harry nodded. "I got used to the name while I was on Earth."

"It's kind of... barbaric, dear," Queen Tamirs said.

"I think it's charming," Zahef said.

His wife shot him a sour look.

Zahef smiled at her innocently. Harry almost laughed. People always said he was a lot like his father, and at times like this, he could see where they were coming from, even though he was the spitting image of his mother.

"Don't be foolish, Zahef'ngh'chaali," his mother told his father. "Harry sounds as simple and barbaric as the names of renegades."

Harry scrunched up his nose.

"It's not at all like their names," Harry said, although he had no idea whether it was true or not. He'd never met a renegade before. "There were human kings called Harry!"

His mother heaved a long-suffering sigh, but Harry knew he'd won.

"Very well—Harry," she said. "Now, will you finally tell us why you want to go back to Sol III?"

Harry shifted from one foot to the other. "I didn't have the time to say goodbye to my friends."

"Friends?" his mother said, her eyebrows flying up. "You made human friends?"

"Why are you saying it as if humans are some sort of animals?" Harry said defensively. "It's not very long before they invent interstellar travel."

"Darling," Queen Tamirs started carefully.

Harry hated, hated, hated it when his mother called him "darling"—it always sounded so condescending, even if it wasn't his mother's intention.

"Darling, by the latest estimates, humans are at least a thousand years away from developing their equivalent of the TNIT," his mother said.

"They'll develop spaceships much sooner than that, though," his father, bless him, cut in. "Perhaps in five hundred years."

"Spaceships are an obsolete technology," Queen Tamirs said with a scoff. "Too slow and ineffective. They don't count. In any case, I don't see why you would want to be friends with members of such a... young civilization."

"Don't Gul'barshyn's teachings say that pride is a sin?" Harry said pointedly.

A faint blush appeared on his mother's cheekbones. She glared.

His father started laughing, earning a flat look from his wife.

"Very good, Harry," his father said, grinning.

Queen Tamirs didn't look amused in the least. "Harht'ngh'chaali," she started.

"Harry," Harry corrected her.

"Harry," his mother conceded, looking pained. "You were sent to Sol III as punishment for your gross violation of another person's mental privacy—"

"I was curious and she's my sister, not just some random person!" Harry said, sulkily. "Sanyash shouldn't have teased me. She knows I can't resist secrets."

"You were sent to Sol III as punishment for your gross violation of another person's privacy," his mother repeated, as if he'd said nothing. "It wasn't a touristic trip. You were meant to learn humility, to learn that your familial links are a privilege, not something to be abused because you're curious."

His mother gave him a look. "You weren't sent to Sol III to make friends with humans. Therefore, I see no reason for you to go back. You wish to say goodbye to your... friends? What would you say, in any case? Humans think extraterrestrial life doesn't exist. You would have to lie to explain your departure."

Harry's shoulders sagged. The worst part was, he knew his mother was right. He couldn't explain to Adam where he was going or why they couldn't even talk on the phone. But—but—

Harry looked at his father pleadingly.

"Maybe it's for the best, Son," his father said gently.

Harry turned around and left the study before he could burst into tears, like the big baby he apparently still was.

He strode toward his rooms, his vision blurring and chest painfully tight as he imagined Adam coming home to an empty flat on his birthday.

How long would Adam wait for him before realizing that Harry was never coming back?

Chapter 9

The flat was empty. Harry wasn't hiding anywhere in order to surprise him with the happy birthday song as Adam had half-expected when he'd come home.

Harry wasn't anywhere.

Adam stared at the table for what felt like the hundredth time since his return home—at the slightly crooked birthday cake on it.

He checked his phone again. No missed calls from Harry, no texts explaining why he wasn't home or where he'd gone. Harry had left his mobile phone in the kitchen.

Adam told himself to stop being such a lovesick worrywart and get a grip. Harry had probably just gone out and lost track of the time. He was worrying over nothing. It had been just a few hours.

Ten hours later, Adam had run out of possible reasons for Harry's absence. He hadn't gotten a wink of sleep last night after realizing that all of Harry's things were still home, including Harry's passport.

It was almost funny.

It was almost funny that he'd learned Harry's last name and nationality from his passport after months of knowing Harry.

Harry Calluvianen. Apparently Harry was a Finn.

It was almost funny. It was almost funny how fast a person could go from happiness to despair and sickening worry.

When he involved the police, there was no longer anything remotely funny about the situation.

"It must be a mistake," Adam said, barely moving his lips.

"There's no mistake, Mr. Crawford," the officer said. "The passport is fake. A very impressive fake, but a fake nonetheless."

Adam turned around and left, already pulling his phone out to call Scott, a friend of his who worked for the MI6. It must be a mistake. Harry wasn't—he wasn't a fucking criminal or something. He'd never believe it.

Six days later, Scott called back and said, "There are no matches in any country. If I didn't know better, I'd say the bloke never existed, Adam."

Adam stared blankly at the hideous painting Harry had bought a month ago. Harry had been so pleased with himself for getting "such a bargain."

Distantly, he heard himself thank Scott before hanging up. Then he got dressed and headed out for work.

"Is everything all right, dear?" Mrs. Wayne, his neighbor, asked him as they shared a lift.

"Yes," Adam said.

"I haven't seen your friend in a week," she said. "The sweet boy promised to look after my flowers while I'm away. Could you remind him about that?"

Adam unclenched his jaw. "He's gone," he said. "He lied to you. All he did was lie."

He barely registered her stunned face as he strode out of the lift without even saying goodbye. She was probably offended by his rudeness, but Adam couldn't bring himself to care.

He didn't care.

Chapter 10

"His Highness Prince Seyn'ngh'veighli of the Third Grand Clan wishes to see you, Your Highness," Borg'gorn announced.

Harry looked up from the 3D model of Earth. He was supposed to be updating the database with the new information he had learned about humans, but instead he'd ended up staring at the 3D model of the planet for something like half an hour. Or rather, at a small island on it.

"Let him in," Harry said belatedly, straightening up and looking at the door. He couldn't wait to see Seyn. They were the same age and had grown up together. Harry had always considered him his closest friend. Seyn was also going to be family in less than two years when he turned twenty-five and his childhood bond to Harry's brother became a marriage bond.

When Harry had returned from Earth, he had been so disappointed to learn that Seyn was off-planet and wouldn't be back for a while. He had wanted to talk to someone he could fully trust and Seyn was the only person he trusted not to judge him.

He smiled when the door slid open and Seyn strode in, as graceful as ever.

Seyn's green eyes lit up when he saw Harry.

"Harht," Seyn said, reaching out with his mind to Harry's.

Suppressing the urge to hug his friend, Harry embraced him back telepathically. Seyn's mind had always felt as silver as Seyn's hair, with a familiar edge of excitement and impatience. Seyn was always in motion, a social butterfly who liked meeting new people and making lots of friends. If he loved, he loved fiercely. If he hated, he hated just as fiercely. Being rather mild-tempered, Harry had always thought it must be exhausting to be Seyn, but lately... he understood him better. Much better.

"I was starting to think you'd been kidnapped by the barbarians on Sol III," Seyn said, grinning.

Harry frowned and gave him a telepathic smack. "Humans are not barbarians. Don't be a snob. And I've been back for ages already. Not my fault you were off-planet."

Seyn scrunched up his nose and smiled sheepishly. "Ugh, I *was* being a snob. Good thing I have you to tell me when I act snobbish and top-lofty."

"Ksar must have rubbed off on you," Harry said with a tiny smirk.

Now it was Seyn's turn to give him a telepathic smack. "Don't even joke about it," he said with a scowl, flopping down on the couch next to Harry. "You have permission to kill me the day I start acting like Ksar."

"Sorry," Harry said, knowing that it was a sore subject for Seyn. He patted Seyn's shoulder. "He's not a monster, you know."

Seyn scoffed.

"He's your brother. Of course you'd say that. Anyway, I'm not here to talk about that asshole." He looked at Harry curiously. "What's wrong, Harht?"

"Harry," Harry said. "I got used to the name and I like it very much."

Seyn just nodded. "So, what's wrong? You're giving off some really negative vibes."

Harry sighed, waved his hand to remove the 3D image of Earth and opened the security settings of the room.

"What are you doing?" Seyn said.

Harry silently turned off the cameras and looked at his friend. "I don't have the bond to Leylen'shni'gul anymore."

"What—Are you serious?" Seyn said, wide-eyed. Of course he was shocked. It was unheard of.

Harry nodded. "I felt it gradually weaken on Earth and then it kind of broke, I think? Just the night before my parents recalled me, actually." He fought a blush, remembering that night, and said quickly, "I thought the bond might rebuild when I returned home, just like my other telepathic links to my family, but it's been twenty-two days and nothing has happened. I don't know what to think."

Seyn was frowning. "Have you talked to Leylen'shni'gul? Does she still feel the bond on her end?"

Harry shook his head. "She's still in that boarding school on Meniiuf II. No communications are allowed unless it's an emergency." He hesitated. "I don't know if I should tell anyone."

Seyn raised his eyebrows. "Why not? I'm sure the mind adepts will just reestablish the bond. I mean, it's been in your mind forever; it shouldn't be hard."

"I..." Harry bit his lip and glanced around the room, paranoid that someone would overhear. "I'm not sure I want the bond back."

Silence.

When Harry dared to look at him again, he found Seyn staring at him.

"Okay," Seyn said slowly. "Who are you and what have you done to my best friend? You always made fun of me when I bitched and whined about my bond to your brother, and now you suddenly don't want the bond, either? You never had a problem with Leylen'shni'gul."

Harry sighed. "It's just..." He ran a hand through his hair. "I feel so much better without it. I feel like I was half-blind all my life. All my senses are better now." It was true. The world felt much more vibrant, the colors brighter, his senses heightened, his telepathy much stronger. He felt better, stronger, *more*. He'd never been against the bond before, but he hadn't known what he'd been deprived of. And now he couldn't imagine going back to that.

On the other hand, if he got bonded again, maybe he would stop feeling so... terribly achy on the inside. Apparently negative emotions were much stronger now, too.

"I don't get it," Harry said. "Why does the bond make our senses worse? We've always been told the bond improved us."

Seyn looked away, his pale brows drawing close.

When he spoke again, his voice was tentative. "I heard some rumors when I was on Planet Bienr last year... I thought they were bullshit, but... maybe they weren't."

"What rumors?"

Still frowning thoughtfully, Seyn played with a lock of his long silver hair. "They have these legends... of the Contact with our ancestors. They were scared of them, Harht. They claimed that some of our ancestors could kill with their minds."

Harry started laughing, but when he noticed how serious Seyn was, the laughter died in his throat. "Surely it's not true?" he said.

Seyn shrugged. "It's been thousands of years. I always thought it was fucking weird that our history books were so hush-hush about the decades between the Great War and the Bonding Law. The Contact with Planet Bienr happened around that time, too."

His brows furrowed, Harry considered it. It was true that the sixty years between the end of the Great War and the introduction of the Bonding Law were barely documented. What was well known was the fact that the biological weapons used in the war affected the population greatly, making women infertile and worsening the quality of men's sperm. Desperate to save the population from going extinct, Calluvian scientists started an experimental genetic program that aimed to fix people's reproductive systems.

It had fixed it, but due to limited testing, there had been unforeseen consequences.

The genetic experiments had caused mutations of various kinds, bringing back extinct physical traits and affecting people's telepathy.

The historical database didn't have much detail, only mentioning that the non-physical mutations disappeared when the Bonding Law had been implemented. According to the Council's reports, the disappearance of the telepathic mutations was just an unexpected side effect of the childhood bond.

"But what does that have to do with the bond dulling our senses?" Harry said, bringing his knees up and hugging them. Since his return home, he found himself constantly craving the comfort of physical touch humans gave so freely.

While Calluvians did touch each other, they did it mostly behind closed doors and far less frequently than humans, preferring telepathic touch. Harry wondered if this newfound craving for physical touch had to do with the absence of the bond. He tried not to think of another reason for his need for physical comfort. Thinking about it *hurt*.

Seyn hummed, looking contemplative. "Telepathy is our sixth sense. If the side effect of the Bonding Law was the disappearance of telepathic mutations, it makes sense the bond affected our other senses, right?"

Seyn's lips thinned. "And when the Council realized that the bond messed with people's senses, of course they kept it hush-hush. That's probably why they force the stupid bond on us so young—babies are too young to remember and notice that something is off." He shook his head. "But it's a bit ridiculous to go to such extreme lengths to protect us from forced bonds, isn't it?"

Harry bit the inside of his cheek as something occurred to him.

Could it be...?

He said slowly, "What if it's a lie that the Bonding Law was introduced to protect us from forced bonds? What if the bond was invented specifically to get rid of the telepathic mutations?"

They stared at each other.

"If you're right..." Seyn said. "If you're right, of course the Council wouldn't care about small side effects like dulled senses as long as the mutations were suppressed too." He sprang to his feet and started pacing the room. "I knew the bond was stupid, but I had no idea it was actually messing up my body in more ways than one." He suddenly stopped and whirled around, facing Harry. "Do you think I can do it, too? Go to a very distant planet like Sol III and get rid of my bond to your ass of a brother that way?"

Harry sighed. It didn't sit well with him when Seyn spoke so ill of his brother. "I don't think it's that simple," Harry said. "If it were that simple, everyone who traveled to distant planets would get their bonds broken."

Seyn shook his head. "The transgalactic teleportation was improved just seventeen years ago. Up until that point, we couldn't travel that far. And you said your bond had broken completely only after months into your stay on Sol III. I don't think any Calluvian ever stayed for so long on such distant planets. Until you."

Harry had to admit Seyn had a point. Up until very recently, they couldn't travel to such distant planets like Earth using teleportation. Their knowledge of Earth had been largely based on what their ally planets that were located closer to Earth knew about it, and the information hadn't been updated in a very long time.

"You can hardly disappear for months," Harry said. "And you have no idea how to survive on Earth."

Seyn waved his concerns away. "If you could do it, I'll manage just fine."

Harry gave him a telepathic smack. "Hey!"

Seyn laughed. "You know I'm right. I'm surprised you didn't get yourself killed or starved. You're too damn naive and kind for your own good."

Harry pouted. "I'm not. I was a very believable human. I learned how to use a coffee-making machine in ten minutes!"

Seyn gave him a blank look. "I have no idea what you just said," he said. "But anyway. It's decided: I'm going to Sol III—I mean, Earth."

Harry sighed at the look of utter determination on Seyn's face. "You know, it upsets me that you hate my brother so much and are willing to do anything to get rid of the bond to him. Why don't you want to become his king-consort? It's a huge honor and you'll really be my family, then."

Seyn's expression softened a little. "Harht, don't take it personally, okay?" he said. "Just try to put yourself in my shoes. Would you want to be bonded for life to such a cold, mean bastard like Ksar? Do you know he never smiles at me? Never! He always looks at me like I'm an annoying little bug beneath his feet. Hell, he ignores me most of the time! That is, unless he's criticizing me for something—"

"But—"

"And that's not all!" Seyn said. "He completely blocks me out of his mind. You know all the stuff people say about the bond being a path to your bondmate's mind? It's bullshit, as far as our bond is concerned. He has never touched my mind.

"Whenever I try to reach out to him, I run into that ugly impenetrable wall that makes me feel dizzy and sick. Why would I want to be bonded for life to such a person?"

Harry sighed. Yeah, he could see where Seyn was coming from. Ksar wasn't much for telepathic affection, even with his family. His mental shields were constantly up and he never let anyone inside.

"If you get your bond dissolved, Ksar will be bondless again," Harry said. "He's been waiting until you reach the age of majority as it is."

Seyn scoffed. "It's hardly my fault his first bondmate died. Lucky girl."

"Seyn!" Harry said reproachfully. "Death is no joke."

Seyn said defensively, "I'm not joking. Death is preferable to the fate of being Ksar's bondmate. I wasn't even born then. It's not my fault Ksar has to wait until I reach twenty-five. He's too old for me anyway."

"He's just eight years older," Harry said. "If you get your bond dissolved, he'll have no other options. Everyone else is matched up."

Seyn didn't look particularly sympathetic. "He can always get bonded to some poor baby and wait until it grows up. It's what they did to me, isn't it?"

Harry sighed and gave up.

It was no use to argue with Seyn about Ksar. And to be totally honest, Ksar didn't make it easy to defend him: he really was extremely cold with Seyn and criticized everything he did.

"Fine," Harry said. "Let's say you found a way to get to Earth and stay there for months. Let's say you got the bond to Ksar dissolved. What are you going to do, then?"

Seyn looked him in the eye and smiled. "I don't know. But I'll be free to make my own choices. I'll be free of him. I'll be free to do whatever I want."

Harry felt a rush of longing so strong it made his chest ache. To do whatever he wanted... It'd been twenty-two days.

"What was that?" Seyn said, frowning at him. "Are you okay?"

Harry took a deep breath, trying to control himself better. He knew he was projecting negative emotions, had been for days.

"I met someone on Earth," he said, looking down at his hands. "We've become... very close. I miss him so much." The words felt so inadequate compared to the ugly, fierce longing that was twisting and hurting his insides.

"Oh," Seyn said. He flopped back on the couch and put an arm around Harry's shoulders. Harry leaned into the touch eagerly, but to his disappointment, the physical comfort did nothing to satisfy the longing eating him from the inside out. He wanted Adam's arms, not Seyn's.

"Wait," Seyn said. "If you aren't bonded anymore, can you feel sexual attraction?"

Harry felt his cheeks burn. He looked at Seyn's eager face. "You're shameless. You shouldn't be wondering about such things."

"Bah!" Seyn said. "As far as I'm concerned, it's natural. It's the stupid bond that turned us into sexless beings." He scowled darkly. "You know, I'm surprised the bond allows us to have sex at all. Actually, if the technology of artificial wombs had already been invented at the time, I'm sure they wouldn't have even bothered to give us back the ability to have sex."

Harry opened his mouth to tell him not to be ridiculous, but he closed it when he realized that Seyn was likely right. The Council had made a single amendment into the Bonding Law fifteen years after the law had been introduced. The bonding ceremony at the age of twenty-five wasn't in the original law. The Council probably hadn't expected that the childhood bond would suppress the brain's sexual arousal centers along with areas affecting telepathy and other senses.

Harry now wondered what the mind adept performing the bonding ceremony did to fix the couple's sexual arousal centers without changing anything else about the bond. It sounded complicated. Was the ability to feel arousal the only difference between the childhood bond and the marriage bond?

"It almost makes me wish the technology of artificial wombs still didn't exist," Seyn said. "Then they wouldn't have bonded me to another male."

Harry rolled his eyes. Of course it was about Ksar. It always was. Seyn never missed the opportunity to bitch about his bond to Ksar and the unfairness of it.

When Harry noticed the curious look Seyn was giving him, he said, "What?"

"Is it true that humans still have such things as heterosexuality and homosexuality?"

Harry nodded. "Heterosexuality is considered the norm there."

Seyn pulled a face. "That sucks. Though, it would be great to be given options instead of being bondmate-sexual. It's a pity your bond broke so late and you didn't get the chance to explore your real sexuality without the bond bullshit."

Harry carefully avoided Seyn's eyes.

"Maybe we should go to Earth together," Seyn said suddenly.

Harry's heart skipped a beat. But he forced himself to shake his head. There was no use getting his hopes up. "Don't be silly. No one would let us go. Don't you think I didn't try? The trips to pre-TNIT planets are regulated by the Ministry of Intergalactic Affairs. Special exceptions can be made, but there must be a very good reason. Considering that the Lord Chancellor of the Calluvian branch of the Ministry is Ksar, good luck trying to convince him that you have a good reason to visit Earth."

"Dammit." Seyn looked at Harry. "Can't you talk to him? He might be a high-handed ass, but he's your brother."

Harry winced. He had been avoiding Ksar as much as he could after his return home. Ksar was too observant. He was a pretty strong telepath, and Harry was scared he'd notice the change in Harry's telepathy—notice that Harry's bond was gone.

"Ksar won't sanction it if there's no good, rational reason," Harry said. "So I didn't even try talking to him about it after my parents said no."

"You still have more chance to convince him than I do," Seyn said. "At least he doesn't hate you."

"He doesn't hate you, either," Harry said unconvincingly. He wasn't actually sure Ksar didn't despise Seyn: he was definitely at his worst around Seyn.

"Right," Seyn said with a snort. "You've always been a terrible liar. I'm surprised that humans didn't suspect anything. I guess you're lucky they don't believe in aliens."

Harry tried to smile but couldn't, suddenly remembering his conversation with Adam about aliens. "Some of them think there are aliens out there, but they don't actually think they look like humans. They have really weird misconceptions about aliens."

"Humans look like us, right? Can I pass for a human?"

Harry eyed Sean critically: his long silver locks, wide green eyes, straight nose, wide mouth. Seyn was taller than average, his body athletic but somehow dainty and graceful too. He was considered very beautiful by Calluvian standards. Harry couldn't say he'd seen a human who looked like Seyn, but then again, he'd seen only a tiny part of Earth.

"I think so," Harry said. "But it doesn't matter. We aren't going to Earth."

Seyn grinned. "Wanna bet?"

Harry should have known better than to bet with Seyn on anything, because seven days later, Seyn sent him a message that said, *"Get ready and come to my house at ten in the evening. We're leaving."*

Harry stared at the message, his heart beating somewhere in his throat.

He was going to Earth.

Chapter 11

"Wanna come with me to Miller's new pub? Heard good things about the place."

"Not tonight, Jake," Adam said, his eyes on his computer screen. "I have work to complete."

"Bullshit," Jake said. "Stanley couldn't praise you enough this morning— said you were ahead on all your deadlines."

Adam continued typing. "I'm busy," he said curtly.

Jake heaved a sigh. "Tell me you aren't going to sleep here again."

"I don't sleep here. It happened a total of two times."

"Look, this isn't healthy, man," Jake said. "First you refuse to leave your place, now you avoid it like the plague."

Adam said nothing, keeping his eyes on the screen.

There was such a long silence he started thinking Jake had left.

"It's been months," Jake said quietly. "He isn't coming back."

Adam clenched his jaw and said nothing.

"Just accept it and move on."

"I have," Adam said, very evenly. "That's why I'm here. Working."

"You aren't working, Adam. You're working yourself to the ground. By the end of the year, you'll be either filthy rich or dead from exhaustion. I'm not sure which is more likely at this point." Jake made an irritated sound. "Forget about that kid. He left without saying goodbye. He's an ungrateful little shit—"

"Get out," Adam said.

"Come on, mate, you know I'm right—"

"Get out," Adam said again. There must have been something ugly in his voice, because Jake flinched and left without saying another word.

When the door shut after him, Adam leaned back in his chair and ran a hand over his tired eyes. Jake was right: he was overworking himself. But work was good. Work kept his mind busy.

Adam pinched the bridge of his nose.

For fuck's sake.

It'd been almost two months. How long was he going to feel like shit? To feel like shit over someone who apparently didn't exist.

It was still hard to believe that everything Harry had told him was a lie, but the facts didn't lie: Harry Calluvianen didn't exist. It almost made Adam think Harry had just been a product of his imagination. Except he wasn't the only one who'd seen Harry. He was real. He had been real.

The thought brought a familiar ache to his chest. Despite his anger, he still couldn't dismiss the possibility that something could have happened to Harry.

People didn't just disappear, especially without taking their passport and possessions with them.

Jake kept telling him to let go, kept telling him that Harry was an ungrateful little shit for leaving like that.

Adam wished he could take that advice, but the problem was, he couldn't completely believe it. After his initial anger and hurt, Adam had thought about their relationship carefully and couldn't believe that Harry—his sincere, sweet, innocent Harry—was actually such a shitty person.

Jake had scoffed when Adam had told him that. "Sincere? Innocent? He lied even about his name! Come on, I know you've got it bad for him, but surely you can't be that blind. He was a fox pretending to be a rabbit, and you bought it."

Jake was right. Rationally, Adam knew it. Irrationally, he kept thinking about the way Harry smiled at him, the way he cuddled into him, the way he trembled under his touch, the way he responded to his kisses, his mouth eager, sweet and so fucking innocent. A person could lie, but the body language couldn't.

Or was he just deluding himself?

Probably. Because no explanation made sense. Adam even considered the possibility that Harry had left because he'd felt guilty for cheating on his fiancée, but that wouldn't explain the fake passport and no identity. Not to mention that Harry wouldn't have baked a goddamn cake for him.

The cake had still been warm when Adam had gotten home. It had been the most maddening thing. He could literally smell Harry's shampoo in the air, as if Harry had just been there.

Jake rolled his eyes every time he tried to argue that Harry couldn't have possibly left of his own volition.

"Unless he was abducted by aliens, there's no excuse for him. Stop being so blind, man! Quit coming up with excuses for the little prick. Forget about him. There's plenty of fish in the sea. What the hell, I don't even recognize you anymore."

Yeah, Jake was right.

He had to be realistic. Harry was a liar. All he had done was lie. Harry—if his name was even Harry—had left and he didn't want to be found.

Maybe the time had come to move on.

Chapter 12

Harry was normally a pretty mild-tempered person, but after the past month, he was very tempted to strangle Seyn. His feet hurt, his legs ached, and he felt gross.

"How was I supposed to know that this stupid planet was so stupidly big?"

Harry said nothing and continued walking. It wasn't the first time Seyn had defended himself even though Harry had never blamed him aloud.

He didn't need to, considering the fact that they had been walking for days from the Port of Grimsby to London.

It was immensely frustrating that they'd wasted an entire month trying to make their way from Los Angeles to London.

To be fair—and Harry wanted to be fair—Harry knew it was partly his fault that he hadn't given Seyn the exact location, assuming that Seyn would tell his friend from planet Touscsse to teleport them to London. But of course Seyn hadn't thought of it. How would Seyn know that Los Angeles was half a planet away from London?

Seyn also had no idea that it would be problematic to travel Earth without Terran documents and money.

Having never been to any pre-TNIT planets, Seyn had been operating under the misconception that Terrans were still stuck in some kind of Middle Ages.

If only Harry hadn't assumed that Seyn would take care of the practicalities. Not for the first time, Harry wished he had his mobile phone or at least could remember Adam's number.

But then again, he wasn't sure he would find the courage to call Adam even if he could.

"We're almost there, anyway," Seyn said, consulting the map in his hand.

"Our parents will kill us," Harry said.

Seyn shrugged carelessly.

Harry told himself to stay calm. They had been traveling for days, and they both were tired and irritable. Fighting wouldn't help anything.

But of course *Seyn* wasn't worried about the wrath of his parents. Seyn had his parents wrapped around his little finger. Seyn could always talk his way out of trouble.

"Ksar will kill us," Harry said.

That finally made Seyn look a bit apprehensive.

But it didn't last long.

"To hell with Ksar," Seyn said. "By the time he finds us, it won't matter. I can barely feel the bond already." He beamed, looking extremely pleased. "Our bond has never been strong; it shouldn't take long now. Anyway, stop worrying."

"Easy for you to say," Harry murmured, dropping his gaze.

Seyn bumped his shoulder against Harry's. "Stop thinking about it. What's done is done. It's not like you enjoyed messing with those humans' minds."

Harry winced.

"I still did it," he said quietly. It didn't sit well with him that he had used his telepathy to trick those humans in New York City into letting them board their ship. The choice of a ship as a means of transport to England had made Harry unhappy enough. If he had to use his telepathy on humans, he would have preferred to use it to get onto a plane, but Seyn had been adamant that he didn't trust "those outdated things" not to crash and kill him.

"We had no choice," Seyn reminded him.

That was true enough. Seyn's communicator didn't work over long distances, which meant they couldn't message Seyn's friend from Touscsse so that the latter could teleport them to the correct location. They had no money and no Terran documents. Telepathy was the only choice.

It didn't make it okay.

"You could have used your telepathy to get us a ride to London," Seyn muttered. "I've never walked so much in my life."

Harry glared at him.

Seyn had the decency to blush. "Just saying!"

"I hated it," Harry said. "I'm not doing it again."

"Personally, I don't think it's a big deal," Seyn said. "You didn't hurt anyone. We just got a free ride on that ship. There was plenty of space for hundreds of people."

"It's the principle of the thing."

Seyn snorted. "I don't remember you being so worried about other people's privacy when you used your familial link to your sister to read her mind. Wasn't it the reason your parents banished you to Earth?"

Harry blushed. "I was curious! And it's different. It's not about privacy. It's about free will. It's not okay to manipulate sentient beings into doing something. Would you want someone to mess with your mind and make you do something?"

Seyn shuddered. "Ugh. You're right. Sorry." He gave Harry a long look. "You're not a Class 1 telepath anymore. You do realize that, right?"

Harry pursed his lips and nodded. "Are you sure your friend won't forget to contact us in three months' time?"

Seyn clearly noticed the change in the subject but didn't comment on it. "Do you think I'm an idiot, Harry?"

Harry smiled a little. At least some good had come from the whole ordeal: Seyn had gotten used to calling him Harry. They hadn't bothered to give Seyn another name, figuring his name sounded human enough.

"No," Harry said. "But I think you're very impulsive and a little irresponsible."

"Irresponsible? Me? At least I didn't escape from my home because I wanted to see some human," Seyn said with a pointed look.

Harry averted his gaze. Of course Seyn was right. While Seyn had a pretty reasonable reason to come to Earth—he wanted to get rid of his unwanted bond— Harry's reason wasn't rational in the least.

He just wanted to see Adam.

He missed Adam *terribly*, in a way he'd never missed anyone else in his life. If he were honest, a month's delay frustrated him so much not because he was afraid of his parents' wrath, but because it had been two months since he'd seen Adam.

Being delayed because of such a trivial reason when he was so close was immensely frustrating.

It didn't help that the more time had passed, the more unsure Harry had felt. Two months was a long time. What if... what if Adam didn't want to see him? What if he was angry?

What if Adam had forgotten about him?

"I'm so curious about that human now," Seyn said. "I don't get why you're so attached to him."

Attached.

Harry imagined being physically attached to Adam—so tightly there was no space between them—and felt a sweet ache spread through his body.

Harry flushed, realizing he was feeling sexual longing in addition to the emotional one.

"He was very kind to me," Harry said awkwardly. He still couldn't bring himself to tell Seyn the whole truth. Being bonded, Seyn wouldn't understand anyway.

"Cheer up," Seyn said. "It shouldn't be long now. We'll be there before sunset."

Harry's heartbeat sped up at the thought of seeing Adam soon. Adam, who would demand explanations, and rightly so.

How was he going to explain his disappearance? How was he going to explain where he had been? And how was he going to explain Seyn's presence?

Would Adam even let him explain?

Chapter 13

Earth wasn't at all like Seyn had imagined. There were so many people, for one thing. It was rare to see such a densely populated planet at this day and age, as most planets had multiple colonies.

What was also extremely rare was seeing his best friend as an anxious wreck. Harry had always been the most positive, relaxed person Seyn had known. But he was unrecognizable as they took the lift to his human friend's flat: Harry was incredibly tense, his body rigid, and he was chewing on his thumb—a childhood habit that used to appear when Harry was extremely nervous and one that Seyn hadn't seen in years.

"Calm down," Seyn said, trying to project reassurance and calmness. "What's there to be nervous about? It's just a human."

"Don't be such a xenophobe," Harry said with a disapproving look, which was what Seyn had aimed for. Harry had needed the distraction.

"I just don't get why you're so nervous," Seyn said with a shrug.

And he really didn't. Harry had been oddly secretive about the Adam person, unwilling to share much, which was weird as hell for Harry. Normally he wouldn't shut up about things he liked.

That was why Seyn was getting increasingly curious about that human.

Finally, the lift doors slid open and Harry headed to the door on the right.

Seyn followed, eyeing his friend with growing concern. Harry was radiating so much anxiety it was starting to affect him too. What was wrong with him?

Harry took an audible breath in and knocked on the door. Was his hand really trembling or was it Seyn's imagination? In any case, anxiety and excitement were rolling off Harry in such strong waves that Seyn took an involuntary step back, uncomfortable.

At last, the door opened.

Seyn stared with interest at the human on the other side. He was tall and classically handsome, with interesting dark eyes, his jaw firm and masculine. He was lovely to look at—or would be if it weren't for the dark circles under his eyes.

The human went rigid when he saw Harry. He didn't even glance at Seyn. His dark eyes zeroed in on Harry.

"Hello," Harry croaked out, his voice shaking.

Seyn looked at him with surprise. But Harry didn't look at him either, his eyes drinking in the human greedily, almost desperately.

The human stared at Harry for what felt like forever, his jaw clenched. "So you're alive. Good to know." His tone was cold and hard.

Harry looked positively crushed.

"Adam," he said, and his voice cracked.

The human swore under his breath, grabbed Harry, and crushed him against his chest.

And Harry... Harry absolutely *melted* into the man's arms with a high, whimpering sound.

Seyn stared.

He watched in confusion as Harry clung to the human, making happy little noises as the human stroked his hair and murmured something into Harry's ear.

He watched the man's hands stroke Harry's back and eventually settle on Harry's lower back. Harry practically purred.

Seyn cleared his throat. "Um, hello?"

The human—Adam—stiffened and lifted his head from where he was nuzzling Harry's hair. He looked over Harry's shoulder at Seyn.

"Who is that?" Adam said.

"It's just Seyn," Harry mumbled, his voice muffled by the human's shirt.

"And who is Seyn?" Adam said, his gaze traveling over Seyn in an assessing manner.

The look made Seyn a bit uncomfortable. Seyn had always been more of an empath than a telepath. He could feel waves of hostility coming off the human without even trying to read his mind.

"He's my childhood friend," Harry said.

Seyn nodded. "I'm going to stay with Harry here for a while."

Adam's eyebrows drew together. "Is that so? And who says Harry is welcome to stay here?"

Seyn thought it was a ridiculous thing to say considering the guy had Harry in a tight embrace.

Harry sighed. He finally stopped clinging to the human and stepped back. "I'm sorry for leaving like that," he said softly, taking the human's hand and looking him in the eye. "I have missed you so much."

Some emotion flickered across Adam's face before it closed off. "Let's talk in the kitchen." He glanced at Seyn briefly. "You can wait in the living room."

Seyn nodded and followed them inside the flat. He flopped down on the couch, content to wait. He wouldn't want to be in Harry's shoes right now. His friend had a lot of explaining to do, and not just to Adam.

Chapter 14

Harry eyed the distance between him and Adam—they were too far apart for his liking—before focusing on Adam's face. It was impossible to read.

Adam said curtly, "Talk."

Harry chewed on his lip.

Adam's gaze flicked to his mouth for a moment before Adam looked back into his eyes. "I'm waiting."

"I don't know what to tell you," Harry admitted.

"The truth would be a good idea," Adam said tersely.

If he could tell Adam the truth, he would have done it ages ago.

Correctly interpreting the miserable look on Harry's face, Adam snorted. "Right." He raked his hand through his hair and turned away, his shoulders and back tense with frustration.

"Is Harry even your name?" he said at last.

Harry's heart skipped a beat. "Yes." For all intents and purposes, he was Harry. Even his parents and best friend called him Harry now.

"Harry Calluvianen doesn't exist," Adam said flatly.

Harry's stomach dropped. So Adam knew his passport was fake.

"Care to explain it?" Adam said. "Apparently, you don't exist." When Harry said nothing, Adam laughed. "Was everything you told me a lie?"

"No!" Harry said, taking a step forward.

He wished he could tell Adam everything, but he and Seyn would be in a lot of trouble for their unauthorized trip to a pre-TNIT planet as it was. If they broke more laws, even their social positions wouldn't save them. There was no hiding anything from the Ministry: there were Dalvars—a species that could detect lies—working for the Ministry and they would know if Harry attempted to lie about it.

"Your passport is fake, Harry."

"Yes, but... I swear, I'm not a criminal or something! I just couldn't use my real name here."

Adam said nothing, his back still to him.

"Please, believe me." Harry walked to Adam and touched his arm tentatively.

"Don't," Adam bit off. "I can't fucking think when you touch me."

Sighing, Harry leaned his cheek against Adam's back and murmured, "If I could tell you the truth, I would, but I can't. It's bigger than me. Bigger than us. I'll break multiple international laws if I do."

Adam gave a harsh laugh. "You sound like a secret agent in a bad spy movie."

Harry smiled. "I'd make an awful secret agent."

Adam heaved a sigh, his muscles relaxing a little. "You have to give me something, Haz."

"I left because my parents sent for me. They didn't give me time to say goodbye. I tried to convince them to let me talk to you, but it was useless."

"So you were home all this time?" Adam said.

"Yes."

"With your fiancée," Adam said without any inflection.

Harry frowned. "No. She's been away at a boarding school."

Silence.

Finally, Adam turned around. He looked Harry in the eye and said, "Is she still your fiancée?"

Harry's breath caught in his throat. He hesitated, unsure how to answer the question—unsure what the answer was.

On one hand, there was no bond anymore.

On the other hand, he hadn't talked to Leylen'shni'gul yet. Until he talked to her, he didn't think answering negatively to Adam's question would be right.

Not to mention that his parents had signed a legally binding betrothal contract on his behalf. Even if the bond was gone, legally he wasn't free.

Harry shrugged a little.

Adam's eyes glinted darkly. "Why did you come back, Harry?"

"I... I missed you," Harry said, a little shy and confused. Wasn't it obvious? He'd already told Adam that.

"But you still have a fiancée back home," Adam said, and there was something very ugly in his tone, some nasty emotion Harry could almost feel despite his tightened mental shields. "Didn't you feel guilty for missing me while you had a fiancée?"

"It's not what you think," Harry said haltingly. "You don't understand."

"That's right," Adam said. "I don't. I don't understand who you are or why you are here, and you know the worst part?" He chuckled humorlessly. "A part of me doesn't give a fuck. I want to keep you, with all your lies and half-truths." He leaned his forehead against Harry's, his hands cradling Harry's face. "What the fuck did you do to me? I should fucking kick you out. I should call the police. I shouldn't still want you."

Harry barely registered his words, heat spreading through his body, delicious and sweet. After months away, having Adam so close was overwhelming.

"You're trembling," Adam said, his fingers stroking Harry's cheek, his neck, making Harry shiver whenever they touched his skin. "Look at you," Adam said, an edge to his voice. "Am I supposed to believe you have a fiancée? You're mine."

Harry couldn't speak, swaying into Adam's touch, and he needed—

"No," Adam said against his ear, his breath harsh and irregular. "Not now. We have your friend waiting in the living room." He removed his hands from Harry and stepped back.

Harry stared at him longingly. Then, his words finally registered. Right. Seyn. He'd completely forgotten about him.

Adam shoved his hands into the pockets of his sweatpants. "Speaking of your friend," he said, clearing his throat a little. He looked pissed off, but when Harry looked down, he could see Adam adjust the bulge in his sweatpants.

Harry licked his lips. "What about Seyn?"

"What is he doing here?" Adam said.

"Seyn helped me escape from home," Harry said before he could stop himself, his mind still foggy with want.

Adam gave him a strange look. "You escaped from home? Why would you need to escape?" He suddenly stiffened, his eyes turning colder. "Harry, is your family... abusive?"

"No!" Harry said quickly. "My parents are just... very traditional. They really want me to marry my fiancée, and I don't want to." Harry dropped his gaze before looking at Adam from under his eyelashes. "I want to be with you, for as long as I can. Can I?"

A mix of conflicting emotions flickered over Adam's face.

"For as long as you can?" he repeated, his expression going blank.

Harry winced, but he was determined to be honest about this.

"I want to stay, but..." Seyn's friend had removed their identification chips and replaced them with temporary ones so that only he could contact them and teleport them back home—if they wanted to go home. That was the one precaution Seyn had gotten right. But it didn't mean they wouldn't be found anyway.

"I can't tell you more than this." Harry met Adam's eyes. "I know it's not enough. I understand if you don't trust me anymore. If you want me to go, I'll go."

Adam's jaw worked. He glared at Harry before suddenly yanking him close, leaning down, and sucking hard on his neck, his mouth hot and possessive.

"You aren't going anywhere," he said harshly before walking out of the room.

Harry stared after him, breathless.

Chapter 15

Adam ordered pizza, because there wasn't anything edible in the kitchen. He'd barely been there since Harry's disappearance, preferring to order a take-out and eat in the living room. Seeing his kitchen empty—seeing all the unnecessary little gadgets Harry had insisted on buying—had made him miserably angry. So he'd avoided the kitchen like the plague.

But now Harry was back.

Harry was back.

Adam could barely take his eyes off him as they ate their pizzas. He had to keep reminding himself that Harry wasn't as innocent and genuine as he appeared, that he shouldn't forgive him so easily. But he couldn't stop staring, hungry for the sight of him.

Their eyes met across the table, and Harry smiled at him, his cheekbones turning a little pink. Adam wanted to kiss them, then lick his way into that pink mouth until Harry was trembling again and making those little noises of his.

"Mmm, this is the best thing I've eaten here! How come you haven't told me about pizza?" Seyn said before taking another bite of pizza and moaning appreciatively.

Harry's nose wrinkled up. "Because I've seen people on the TV say it's unhealthy to eat it."

Adam watched them with bemusement. He had thought Harry's odd obliviousness about so many obvious things was just a quirk of his, but his friend seemed to share it. Seyn was as weird as Harry.

And just like Harry, he seemed like a character that had escaped from a Disney fairy tale. He was ethereally beautiful with unnaturally white skin, long silver hair, and deep green eyes. He looked like a freaking prince. There was also something… off about his looks. It wasn't the hair color; Seyn wasn't the first bloke Adam had seen who dyed his hair into strange colors.

No, it was something else. Some quality that Harry had too.

"So how long are you staying here?" Adam said, glancing at Seyn.

Seyn paused mid-chew. He exchanged a long look with Harry. It almost seemed as though they were communicating without speaking. They must have been really close.

"I hope it's okay for me to stay with you guys until I find a job," Seyn said and took a sip of tea.

Adam suppressed a snort. It would be impossible for him to answer negatively without looking like a prick. This guy wasn't as socially clueless as Harry tended to be.

"You'll have to share with Harry," Adam said. "There's no spare room. Unless you want to sleep on the couch."

"He can take my room," Harry said, glancing at Adam from under his eyelashes. "I can share with you."

Adam wet his lips and gave a clipped nod.

Harry dropped his gaze again.

In the meantime, Seyn choked on his tea and started coughing, his eyes wide as saucers. "You're going to share a bed with Adam?" he said, looking at Harry like he'd grown a second head.

Harry eyed his pizza like it was the most interesting thing in the world. "I'd rather share a bed with Adam than with you. You don't even know how to cuddle."

Seyn stared at him with a vaguely scandalized look. Adam would have laughed if he weren't busy trying not to show how much the mere idea of Harry sleeping in his bed affected him.

Sleeping. Right.

"Okay," Seyn said, giving Harry the "we'll talk later" look.

"So how long have you known each other?" Adam said, taking pity on Harry, who looked like he was about to burst into flames. It shouldn't have been so endearing. Christ, it was fucking impossible to stay angry with that face.

"Pretty much forever," Seyn said, making Adam flinch and tear his eyes away from Harry.

When he looked back at Seyn, he found him studying him curiously.

Right. He had asked Seyn a question.

"Really?" Adam said, after clearing his throat.

"Our parents are old friends and his older brother is my fiancé, so we were kind of forced to socialize," Seyn said.

He grinned. "If we weren't, I wouldn't have been friends with such a naive cupcake. I'm surprised he didn't get himself killed while he was all on his own here."

"I'm not that hopeless," Harry said with a pout. "Stop exaggerating."

"Wait," Adam said. "Seyn is engaged to your brother? You told me I was the first gay person you'd ever met."

Harry's eyes widened. He exchanged a panicked look with Seyn.

"I'm not gay," Seyn said. "I'm—I'm—bisexual—"

"Demisexual!" Harry said at the same time.

They glared at each other.

Adam smiled without mirth. "You should have made an effort to coordinate your stories."

Harry dropped his face into his hands and groaned. "I didn't lie to you," he mumbled into his hands. "You really are the first homosexual person I've ever met. Seyn's sexuality is... complicated." He peeked at Adam through his fingers. "You're angry at me, aren't you?"

He should have been.

But despite Harry's blatant lies, they didn't seem malicious—or perhaps Adam was a terrible judge of character.

"Of course I'm angry," Adam said. He was, but mostly at himself for not being angry enough. He might not be as angry at Harry as Harry's constant lying deserved, but it didn't mean it was okay.

Because it *wasn't* okay. Part of him couldn't believe he was ready to forgive Harry so easily. If it were anyone else, he would have told them to fuck off. He wouldn't have even let them into his flat.

Harry's face fell.

"Oh for the love of— He doesn't hate you, Harry!" Seyn said, getting to his feet with an exasperated huff. "I don't get why you get so stupid around this—man." He fake yawned. "Anyway, I'm tired. Show me your room?" he said, shooting Harry a meaningful look.

Harry didn't even glance at him, his eyes still on Adam. "You really don't hate me?"

"Harry," Seyn said impatiently.

"I don't," Adam said and sighed. "Go. Show him your room, babe."

Harry's face lit up. "I'm still your babe?"

Adam smiled, remembering Harry's adamant insistence on being his only babe, whatever that meant. "If you want to be."

Harry was out of his chair and on his lap in an instant. "I want to," he murmured into Adam's ear, his body pressing tightly against Adam's. "Want to be your babe. Always."

Adam felt his body stiffen in response. He pulled Harry tighter to him and mouthed the soft skin under his ear, breathing him in. Fuck, he couldn't be angry with him.

Harry let out a happy sigh. "I missed this so much," he said, his voice raw with honesty. "Your arms around me. You."

"Yeah," Adam murmured. Fucking hell, had he missed him. Harry's scent, the way he fit against Adam's body, the heady mix of desire and adoration that filled his body whenever they touched: he'd missed all of that.

Harry buried his fingers in Adam's hair, pushing Adam's mouth closer to his neck, his breathing coming in short gasps.

Adam sank his teeth into Harry's skin, sucking gently.

Harry gasped and tilted his head to the side, giving him better access, his fingers roaming up and down Adam's biceps as Adam covered his neck in marks. Harry. His baby, his angel, his favorite human being, his pretty boy—

A choked sound made Adam remember they had an audience.

Stiffening, Adam looked over Harry's shoulder, his mouth still pressed to Harry's delicate neck.

Seyn was staring at them, wide-eyed.

"Harry," Seyn said. "A word."

Harry didn't move from Adam's lap.

"Now," Seyn said.

Harry looked at Adam longingly.

"Harry!" Seyn gritted out. "I need to talk to you. Now."

Harry sighed and climbed off Adam's lap. "I'll come back soon," he said, his eyes soft and glazed over.

Adam nodded, watching them go and suppressing the paranoid urge to grab Harry and never let him out of his sight.

He sagged back in his chair and sighed. For fuck's sake, Harry was just going to another room.

Adam glanced at his watch. It was fast approaching midnight and he had to get up early tomorrow. A shower sounded like a good idea while Harry talked to his friend.

Chapter 16

"Are you out of your mind?" Seyn said as soon as they entered Harry's old room. "If I'd known about this, I would've never taken you to Earth with me."

Harry's stomach lurched with nerves. He crossed his arms over his chest. "I don't know what you're talking about."

Seyn gave him a telepathic smack.

Harry tightened his mental shields and glared at him.

Seyn glared back. "Don't play dumb. What are you doing, Harry?"

Harry averted his gaze. "I don't know what you mean."

"Right." Seyn sighed. "You know it's hopeless. No matter how attached you are to this human, you'll never be allowed to be yourself with him. You'll never be allowed to stay here. We aren't allowed to stay indefinitely on pre-TNIT worlds."

"No one knows where we are except for your friend," Harry said tightly.

"Don't kid yourself. They may not know now, but eventually they'll find out." Seyn shook his head, looking at him with such pity it turned Harry's stomach.

"Don't get too attached to him, Harht. Try to keep some reasonable distance. You're way too *affectionate* with him already." Seyn gave him a pointed look. "Was it really necessary to sit on his lap and let him kiss your neck? Is it another human custom I wasn't aware of?"

Harry blinked. Had Seyn really not realized that his relationship with Adam was less than platonic? Was he genuinely oblivious? It was hard to believe. But then again, Seyn was bonded, and the areas of his brain responsible for sexual attraction were suppressed by the bond. For all of Seyn's bold talk, he had no experience when it came to sex and relationships. Seyn had no idea what attraction felt like. Maybe he couldn't recognize it.

Harry almost envied him. Things had been so much easier when his body didn't behave so strangely, drawn to Adam like a magnet. He had been addicted to Adam's touch and Adam's attention long before his bond had broken, but now it was so much worse. Now there was another dimension to his feelings, one that was harder to suppress.

"Promise me you'll put some distance between him and you," Seyn said, looking at him intently.

"I promise," Harry said, feeling like the worst sort of liar. He would try his best, but he knew he was too weak where Adam was concerned.

To Harry's relief, after that Seyn changed the subject. Seyn spent the next hour asking Harry about human customs and some things Adam had mentioned that confused him. Finally, after what felt like forever, he let Harry go. Harry took a quick shower in the ensuite and changed into fresh clothes, happy to find that Adam hadn't removed Harry's clothes from his wardrobe.

By the time he left his old room, the rest of the flat was already dark.

Harry pushed the door to Adam's bedroom open and padded inside. Adam had left the French windows open and the moonlight illuminated the room pretty well. Coupled with Harry's much improved eyesight, he could see everything perfectly.

Adam seemed fast sleep, his chest rising and falling evenly. He was only in his boxers.

Harry tore his eyes away and undressed to his underwear as quietly as he could. He was a little disappointed that Adam was asleep, but maybe it was for the best. He didn't think he could keep his promise to Seyn if Adam was awake and they picked up where they left off.

Harry slipped into bed and rolled onto his side, facing Adam.

He stared at Adam's handsome profile and felt his throat close up.

Adam was human. In the dark and quiet of the night there was no escaping that fact.

Adam was human.

And Harry very much wasn't.

Harry might hate it, but Seyn's concerns were valid. His relationship with Adam had an expiration date. He wouldn't be able to stay on Earth indefinitely. Sooner or later, he and Seyn would be found and deported.

His family would never let him stay with Adam even if the Ministry weren't in the picture. His parents would never approve or accept his relationship with Adam. They would likely be horrified.

Adam was human, a member of a pre-TNIT civilization.

While Harry thought humans were interesting and really fascinating, he was well aware of the fact that people back home didn't share his opinion.

At best, pre-TNIT civilizations were looked down on.

At worst, they were despised. Having an intimate relationship with a member of a pre-TNIT civilization was unheard of. In the eyes of society, such a relationship would be considered no better than modern humans would regard a relationship with a Neanderthal.

As far as Harry knew, even before entering the Union of Planets and becoming subject to the Ministry's laws, his planet had very few relations with pre-TNIT civilizations. Calluvians took pride in being one of the oldest civilizations in the galaxy and tended to look down on younger civilizations like Earth.

Harry had always thought that such attitude was in extremely poor taste, but he was aware that most people back home thought differently. His parents said he was naive. His sister said he was too idealistic. Ksar said he was too soft.

They would never understand or approve.

Swallowing, Harry moved closer to Adam, just a little.

Adam frowned in his sleep, his brows knitting together before his eyelids fluttered open.

"Haz?" he muttered, reaching for Harry. "C'mere."

Harry rolled over until his face was against Adam's bare shoulder. He was so relieved Adam didn't seem to be angry with him anymore.

"What time is it?" Adam said, a hoarse layer of sleep still in his voice.

"Twenty minutes past one o'clock," Harry replied, closing his eyes.

He dragged his nose over the curve of Adam's biceps, inhaling deeply. "I love your scent so much. I missed it. Nothing smells as good as you."

Adam snorted. "I'm sure there's something that smells better."

Not to me.

Harry shook his head. There was something about Adam that made him feel so…primitive. When he was with Adam, he didn't feel like a prince of an ancient civilization. He felt like a slave to his body and its impulses. He felt like shoving his face into Adam's armpit and breathing in his masculine scent and sweat. *Mine. My man.* He felt like begging Adam to mark him up everywhere. He felt like Adam's, in every possible way.

A crooked smile twisted Harry's lips. "I want to smell of you so much I think I'd happily let you piss on me." He was joking. Mostly.

Adam gave a strained laugh. "You can't just say stuff like that."

"Why not?" Harry said, kissing Adam's shoulder softly.

"Because I'm just a red-blooded man," Adam bit out. "And you're engaged to someone but say you want to *smell* of me. Do you realize how it looks, Harry?"

"Pretty bad?" Harry said, rubbing his warm cheek against Adam's shoulder. He did understand that from Adam's point of view, Harry was engaged to someone, had a romantic relationship with someone, so it was wrong of him to want Adam.

But it wasn't like that.

Harry wished he could explain it to Adam, but he didn't know how.

Adam wasn't Samantha. He couldn't tell Adam that it was an arranged marriage without Adam asking more uncomfortable questions—questions he couldn't answer honestly.

"You probably think I'm a terrible person," Harry said. *He* would think he was a terrible person if he were in Adam's place and had the same limited information Adam did.

Adam heaved a sigh. "I just can't reconcile things I know about you with things I see."

"What do you see?"

Adam propped himself on an elbow, facing Harry.

They were so very close.

Harry wet his lips, his heart thudding hard against his rib cage. He put his hand on Adam's chest. Adam's heart was beating fast, too, his skin warm under Harry's palm. Human body temperature was a little higher than that of Calluvians, and Adam always felt wonderfully warm. He felt even warmer now.

"I see…" Adam trailed off, his knuckles stroking Harry's cheek, then down his neck.

Harry shivered, goosebumps running over his skin. He leaned into Adam's touch, sucking a breath in when Adam's hand moved down his chest. He moistened his lips and stared at Adam's mouth hungrily, a now-familiar need stirring in his body. He *wanted*. He wanted to attack Adam's mouth with his: kiss it, bite it, and lick into it. He wanted to yank Adam on top of him, spread his legs and beg Adam to make him feel good with his cock, like last time.

When Adam's hand moved to stroke his quivering stomach, Harry couldn't take it anymore.

"Let's have sex," he blurted out. "I want to have sex with you. So much."

Adam made an odd, strangled noise that sounded like half-laugh, half-groan, his body stiffening, his muscles almost vibrating with tension. "Haz—"

"Please," Harry said, slipping his hand into Adam's boxers and pulling out his cock. He stroked it greedily. It felt amazing in his hand, both hard and kind of silky.

A part of him couldn't believe his own boldness. That part of him told him to be ashamed of how much he wanted it—wanted to have actual sex with someone who wasn't his bondmate, with a member of another species, with a man Harry's race would consider little better than a barbarian.

But that part of him was very small and grew weaker with every passing minute. Harry didn't care. He didn't care what people back home would think of him if they could see him now. He wanted Adam, wanted everything he could get, wanted to have Adam inside him—wanted Adam to *fuck* him. The word "fuck" had always seemed dirty and vulgar to Harry, both in Calluvian and Terran languages, but now he thought it fit the base want burning his body. He wanted to be fucked. He wanted Adam to fuck him. He wanted it with a desperation that was worsened by the knowledge that his time with Adam was limited.

"Let's have sex," Harry said, squeezing Adam's cock. "I want you so much."

Adam cursed and suddenly rolled on top of him, pinning him to the mattress with his long, heavy body. Adam's thigh pressed between his legs, against his hard cock. Harry whimpered.

Wrapping his legs around Adam's hips, he surged up and kissed Adam clumsily, licking into his mouth.

Adam groaned and returned the kiss, his tongue thrusting into Harry's mouth in a rhythm Harry longed for him to do with his body. Squirming, Harry ground against Adam's cock, trying and failing to relieve the ache in his groin. "Adam," he whispered against Adam's mouth.

"What, babe?" Adam murmured between the long, wet, dizzying kisses.

"I need," Harry said, squirming fruitlessly under Adam, trying to pull him closer. "Need you."

Adam turned his head to mouth at Harry's ear, his breathing unsteady. "What do you need, Haz?"

Harry's brows furrowed. Hadn't he made it clear already? "Need you to fuck me."

Adam drew in a harsh breath. "Are you sure?" he said, his voice so deep it was nearly unrecognizable.

Harry nodded dazedly, gripping Adam's buttocks. "Want to feel you inside me."

Adam made a low, growling sound before dragging his wet mouth down Harry's neck. "Yeah," he rasped, sucking love bites into Harry's skin. "We just need—" Adam tore himself away with a muffled curse and reached out for the drawer. He rummaged in it for a few moments before swearing again. "I have condoms, but I'm out of lube."

Harry blinked at him, unsure what he was talking about. "Doesn't matter," he mumbled, trying to pull Adam back onto him.

Adam laughed harshly. "We need lube, Haz. I need to prepare you, to open you up for my cock."

Adam's cock.

Harry shivered, his own cock throbbing and his hole leaking, so empty. He shook his head. "I don't need it," he managed. "I'm ready, I swear."

He could see Adam's frown as he peered at him in the darkness. "Harry—"

"I'm ready," Harry nearly whined, grabbing Adam's hand and shoving it in his underwear. Bypassing his hard cock, Harry pressed Adam's fingers against his slick hole and whimpered at the contact.

Adam drew in a sharp breath. "Did you prep yourself for me before coming to bed?" He pushed a finger in and Harry shuddered. Yes, this was what he had needed so badly. Distantly, he realized that Adam was asking something and nodded, hoping it was the correct response. He didn't care—as long as Adam kept him filled up.

Adam stroked the inside of Harry's hole with two fingers, scissoring them. It felt so good, but it wasn't enough. Harry wanted more. Harry wanted—he wanted… He looked at Adam's cock, standing thick and long, and his hole clenched around Adam's fingers.

"Want," Harry said, reaching down and grabbing Adam's cock's again. It was even harder now. Harry whined, imagining how good it would feel, filling him up and stretching him to the limit. "Put it in."

Adam swore under his breath, knocked Harry's hand away, and quickly rolled something on his cock.

"Spread your legs for me, baby," he said, settling between Harry's thighs.

Harry did and watched impatiently as Adam guided his cock inside him. Harry let out a quiet, blissful sigh as the hard length filled him slowly. Too slowly. Frowning, Harry moved his hips, trying to get it deeper.

Adam hissed. "Haz, slow down. You'll hurt yourself." Despite his rational words, he sounded *gone*, his hands stroking Harry's thighs and his cock starting to move inside Harry.

"Don't want slow," Harry managed, moaning as Adam started thrusting harder. "Feels good. I didn't know sex would feel so good."

Adam let his weight press Harry into the mattress. "I'm your first," he muttered into Harry's neck, gripping Harry's thighs hard as he slammed into him. "No one's ever done this to you. Just me. Just mine."

The possessiveness in Adam's voice sent an insane thrill through Harry's body. Panting, he moved to meet Adam's thrusts. He wanted more, harder, deeper, but for some reason, Adam kept changing the angle and length of his thrusts. Harry whined in frustration, clutching at Adam's back, trying to pull him deeper.

"Shhh," Adam said. "Or your friend will hear us."

Harry flushed, remembering that Seyn was on the other side of the wall. But his embarrassment didn't stop him from wanting more of Adam's cock, and he keened, meeting Adam's thrusts, his hole clenching on Adam's cock. It felt so good inside him, so very good, thick and perfect, but he wanted more.

"Fuck, I can't find your prostate," Adam grated out, muscles tense and brows knitted in concentration as he continued changing the angle of his thrusts.

"Prostate?" Harry croaked, not understanding.

"Christ." Adam half-laughed half-groaned, lips dragging over Harry's neck as his cock pistoned in and out of Harry. "I feel like I'm robbing the cradle. But I want—you—so—badly."

Each word was punctuated by a hard thrust. "Touch yourself, baby," Adam said. "Stroke your cock for me. You're so pretty, so beautiful—feel so wonderful."

Harry practically preened from the praise. He did as he was told, slipping his hand between them and grabbing his neglected cock. The relief was immediate. He let out a long moan and started moving his hand hard and fast, at the same rhythm as Adam's thrusts. But he still needed more.

"Harder," he whispered brokenly, squeezing Adam's back with his legs. "Want harder—need—please." He was so, so slick, aching from the inside, sobbing out every time Adam pulled out his cock. He knew it wouldn't hurt no matter how rough Adam was with him; he just wanted harder and deeper. "More!"

Adam pulled out, making him whine. He put Harry on his hands and knees before slamming back into him, deep and hard. Harry cried out, his eyes moistening. Yes, right there. It felt so good, so satisfying. He no longer cared that Seyn could likely hear him, moaning wantonly with each deep thrust. Adam was groaning, too, the mattress creaking under them, the headboard knocking against the wall with the force of Adam's thrusts.

"God, fuck fuck fuck," Adam growled, biting at Harry's back, his hand closing around Harry's cock and pumping it hard. "So fucking tight, so good, so perfect for me—" His cock hit something inside him.

Harry sobbed out and felt his world explode, immense waves of pleasure rocking his body and stealing his breath away.

He fell on the mattress, feeling boneless, his head spinning with pleasure.

He could feel Adam's hands roving over his skin, petting, stroking, guiding him through the aftershocks, even as Adam continued thrusting into him. Although Harry felt sated, Adam's thrusts still felt good and he kind of didn't want Adam to ever stop.

But he stopped eventually, groaning, his body stiffening on top of him.

Harry sighed in disappointment when Adam pulled out. "You could've stayed in me."

Adam chuckled, rolled onto his back and pulled Harry into his arms. "Insatiable," he muttered, his voice already sleepy. "Never thought you'd be such a handful in bed."

Harry didn't know what to say to that. Was it bad? Or was it a compliment?

Before he could ask, he felt Adam's drift off to sleep.

Smiling, Harry buried his face in Adam's armpit and did the same, feeling safe and loved in Adam's arms. Home. This felt like home.

Chapter 17

Adam had always thought it was kind of creepy to watch someone sleep. He'd never understood the urge to do so.

But that morning, as he watched Harry sleep with his cheek on his chest, Adam fully understood the sentiment. He couldn't drag his eyes away. He wasn't sure he could drag his eyes away for all the money in the world.

Harry looked even lovelier when he slept, his porcelain skin a striking contrast to his dark eyelashes and chestnut hair—and Adam's tanned chest.

He was so damn beautiful.

And he was his.

Really? said a snide voice at the back of his mind that sounded a lot like Jake's. *You don't even know if his name is really Harry. You know shit about him. Except for the fact that he has a fiancée back home.*

Adam pressed his lips together.

It was true that there were too many things about Harry that just didn't add up.

He was so innocent and naive at times that it was hard to believe Harry was capable of lying—lying to him for months. And if Harry really had a fiancée, what did it say about him as a person that he was so eager for Adam's cock? Or about Adam, for that matter. He'd always thought he was a better man than that.

And then there was the sex. It had been…

Trying to ignore his morning wood, Adam forced himself to think about the sex rationally.

Last night there had been something that niggled at the back of his mind, but his arousal had prevented him from thinking about it.

The fact that Harry had prepared himself for anal sex before coming to bed was so out of character for him. That was the same person who blushed at innuendos, the same person who didn't know what a prostate was. And Adam was supposed to believe Harry had stretched and slicked himself so thoroughly he'd remained wonderfully slick throughout the sex. So, either Harry was pretending to be naive and inexperienced, or...

What was the alternative?

"Good morning."

Adam snapped his eyes back to Harry and found him blinking blearily with a soft, sleepy smile.

Christ, Adam wanted to fucking consume him, kiss him from his sleep-tousled head to his flawless pale toes.

"Morning," Adam said, clearing his throat a little. "Sleep well?"

Harry nodded, yawning. "I haven't slept this well in ages."

"Good," Adam said, leaning in.

His alarm went off, making him pause.

Fuck. Work. If he started kissing Harry now, he would definitely be late.

Sighing, Adam extracted himself from Harry's arms and rolled off the bed, stoically ignoring Harry's pout.

"I need to be at work earlier than usual," Adam said with a grimace, grabbing a fresh pair of boxers and heading quickly toward the ensuite bathroom.

He paused, noticing a strange expression on Harry's face. "Everything okay?"

Harry lowered his lashes. "I just... I already miss you. I don't want you to go." He chuckled, rubbing the back of his neck. "I know it's silly."

Adam wished he could laugh it off and tell Harry he really was being silly, but truth be told, at the back of his mind, there was still the persistent fear that Harry would disappear again. No matter what he told himself, he couldn't completely convince himself that he wouldn't come home to an empty flat that evening.

"It's not silly, love," Adam said, laughing inwardly at his own clinginess. If half a year ago someone told him he'd have it so bad for someone, he would have called them crazy. "I already miss you, too."

Harry beamed at him. Adam had to forcibly drag his eyes away and make his feet move toward the ensuite. Christ. He felt like a teenager with his first crush. What had that boy done to him?

By the time he emerged out of the bedroom, fresh out of the shower and dressed for work, he found Harry in the kitchen, frowning at the contents of the fridge.

"There's no food," Harry said. "So I'm heating up the leftover pizza." He turned to Adam with a puzzled look. "Why don't you have food?"

Adam didn't answer. He walked over to Harry, crowded him against the fridge and slotted his lips against Harry's. Harry trembled and opened his mouth eagerly, turning the gentle kiss into a dirty one as he sucked on Adam's tongue with happy little noises. It made Adam imagine what noises Harry would make with a mouth full of his cock, and he groaned, kissing Harry harder.

Someone cleared their throat.

Harry jumped away from Adam, pink-cheeked and breathless—and so beautiful. It took an effort to look away from him. But look away he did.

Seyn was staring at them, his eyes darting from Harry to Adam and back. There was a very strange expression on his face as Seyn bored his eyes into Harry. Harry, who seemed to be studiously avoiding Seyn's gaze.

"Pizza!" Harry said, turning to the microwave.

Adam noted with slight bemusement that Harry continued to avoid Seyn's eyes throughout breakfast. In fact, Harry barely spoke to Seyn while Seyn spent most of the time staring at Harry like he'd grown a second head. It almost seemed as though he was trying to communicate something to Harry, but Harry either hadn't noticed or decided to ignore it.

"Hey, Adam," Seyn said, finally shifting his gaze to Adam's face.

Adam poured himself a cup of coffee and looked at him. "What?"

Seyn bored his eyes into Adam's. Suddenly, a dull headache started building in his head and Adam frowned, rubbing at his temples. He usually wasn't one to get headaches.

"Seyn!" Harry said sharply.

Seyn flinched, but Adam didn't pay him attention anymore. He stared at Harry. He'd never seen Harry angry, much less furious. But he was undeniably furious now, flushed and glaring daggers at his friend, who was looking guilty and defensive all of a sudden. What in the world... These two were so fucking strange.

"Don't do that," Harry bit off, still glowering at his friend.

"All right, what's going on?" Adam said, getting more than a little fed up with all the secrecy between these two. At least his headache was gone.

"Nothing," Seyn said after a long moment of him and Harry glaring at each other. He sighed. "You're making a huge mistake, Harry," he said, his voice softer now. "Your parents will kill you." He chuckled, shaking his head. "I had no idea you had it in you. Is that even legal to do that with him when you're..."

Harry blushed and sprang to his feet. "You're going to be late for work if you don't go now," he told Adam, grabbing his arm.

Adam frowned and glanced at Seyn, who had an almost pitying expression on his face as he looked at Harry.

"Adam, come on," Harry said. "I'll explain later."

Adam studied him.

Harry was chewing on his lip, his violet eyes wide and pleading.

"Fine," Adam said, letting go. But only because he didn't have the time now.

He would demand answers in the evening.

Enough was enough.

He was tired of secrets and lies.

Chapter 18

"Don't," Harry said as soon as they were alone in the flat.

Seyn shook his head. "Harry—"

"And don't you dare do that to Adam again," Harry said, glaring at him. "It was a violation of his privacy. You had no right to read his mind."

Before Seyn could say anything, Harry turned and disappeared into Adam's room.

Seyn sighed and massaged his head, trying to get rid of the headache that he had developed when Harry gave him a massive telepathic blow for prying into Adam's mind. Seyn still wasn't used to how strong Harry's telepathic abilities had become after his bond had broken. Seyn had always been the stronger telepath and empath between the two of them, and their role reversal took him aback. Sure, Seyn had witnessed Harry use his newfound powers on humans, but being on the receiving end of them was different. For the first time, Seyn felt a little unnerved. He now understood better why Harry was so disturbed by his increased abilities.

Telepathic races had always been regarded with certain wariness and suspicion by other races in the galaxy. But everyone knew not all telepaths were equally dangerous.

The Standard Telepathic Test was invented by the Ministry to classify telepaths, with Class 1 the most harmless and Class 7 the most dangerous. Harry had been a Class 1 telepath on the STT, the weakest telepathic class besides t-nulls, but Seyn's head was still ringing from the force of Harry's telepathic blow—and he had his mental shields on! Harry was at least Class 3 now. At the very least.

It made him a little uneasy, because Seyn was classified as Class 2 even with the bond restricting his telepathic core. He tried not to think how he would be classified on the STT when his bond to Ksar finally broke. He also tried not to think about the ancient Calluvians who could kill with their minds. It was probably a bullshit urban legend, but if it was true... those mutants would have been classified as Class 7.

Seyn pushed the thought away with a chuckle. He was being silly. Class 7 telepaths no longer existed in the galaxy. Everyone knew that.

He had more pressing things to worry about anyway.

Like the fact that his best friend had clearly lost his mind.

Seyn felt his skin go warm as he remembered what he had seen in Adam's mind before Harry shoved him out of it. Even with Adam's memories and all the noise he had heard last night, it was still hard to believe Harry had really engaged in... sexual intercourse with his human.

Harry had had *sex*.

There was a part of Seyn that gleefully cheered Harry on for going against all the archaic stifling traditions of their people. That part of him was immensely curious about what it felt like. That part of him was determined to try the sex thing as soon as his stupid bond finally broke. But, unlike Harry, he had no intention of becoming so besotted with a member of a pre-TNIT civilization.

How could Harry be so stupid? He was already too attached to his human. Adding sex on top of that was a terrible idea.

Seyn might not entirely understand romantic love, but he had a good idea what it was like from his friends from other planets. If he understood it correctly, intense attachment and sexual attraction were the main components of romantic love for sexual sentient beings.

Harry had already been too attached to his human. Adding sex into the mix had exponentially increased his chances of getting hurt when their parents inevitably found them and dragged them home. The Ministry's laws forbade them to have a permanent residence on pre-TNIT planets. Harry and his human had no future.

Seyn shook his head. He didn't know what Harry was thinking.

If he was thinking at all.

Sighing, Seyn walked to Adam's room and knocked shortly before pushing the door open.

Harry was sprawled on his back on the bed. His eyes flicked to Seyn and a frown appeared on his face. But he said nothing, waiting for Seyn to speak first.

Seyn walked over and sat on the bed.

They looked at each other.

"You know, when I was on planet Sivaxu last year," Seyn started. "They tried to teach me their ways. They were not religious, but they were believers. They believed that everyone had a path written in the stars. That no matter what you did, you couldn't change your path in a significant way if the change wasn't already written in the stars."

Harry pursed his lips. "I don't understand."

"You know it can't end well," Seyn said carefully. "He's a human and you're you. You know it's hopeless. He has his own path to travel, Harry. You were never meant to cross it or change it. End it before it's too late. He's not for you. He's not yours and he'll never be yours."

Harry dropped his gaze, his long dark eyelashes suspiciously moist against his pale cheeks. It made Seyn's chest hurt, but he knew the words needed to be said. Harry was such a gentle soul. He tended to ignore the harsh reality, determined to believe in the best outcome, no matter how unrealistic it was.

"You think it's so easy?" Harry whispered tightly. "To turn off your emotions? To end things when all you want is him?"

Seyn opened his mouth and closed it without saying a word. The truth was, he really had no idea what Harry was going through. He had no idea what wanting to be with someone felt like. And he was so, so curious.

Seyn nudged Harry's knee. "What is it like?" he said, adopting a lighter tone. He'd done his duty and warned Harry; he was allowed to indulge his curiosity.

Harry blinked and then blushed when Seyn smirked.

"Come on, Harry," he said. "Spill! Is sex as good as they say?"

"It's very private, don't you think?"

"Oh come on!" Seyn said, pouting. "It wasn't very private when you were moaning and begging Adam to do you harder last night."

Harry flushed and covered his face with a pillow. "Shut up!"

Seyn grinned. "What? I have ears! It's not my fault you're such a whore in bed!"

Harry kicked him. "I hate you," he mumbled into his pillow. "And maybe you're more of a whore in bed than me. You just don't know it yet." Harry lifted his pillow off his face and smiled innocently at Seyn. "I'll ask Ksar after your wedding night."

That little shit.

Harry started giggling at the look on Seyn's face.

"Never going to happen," Seyn bit off, lifting his chin.

Over his dead body.

Chapter 19

Harry genuinely tried to wait for Adam's return from work, but he was a needy mess of emotions by eleven o'clock. Seyn's earlier words—that Adam wasn't really his and would never be his—formed a knot of anxiety in the pit of his stomach. He wanted to see Adam.

That was how he ended up in Adam's office before lunch.

In the hindsight, it probably wasn't his best idea.

Leaning against the desk in Adam's office, Harry tried to ignore Jake and Adam's conversation.

He tried.

Really.

But with his heightened senses, their hushed argument wasn't hushed to him at all. He couldn't help but overhear it.

"Are you fucking kidding me, man?" Jake hissed furiously, glaring at Harry over his shoulder before turning back to Adam. "You're forgiving him? Just like that?"

Adam was leaning his shoulder against the far wall, his arms crossed over his chest. His posture was relaxed and confident, but his narrowed eyes betrayed that he was anything but relaxed.

His shoulders looked so amazing in that blue shirt, the fabric accentuating the width of them.

Harry squirmed. Since they'd had sex—or perhaps, since his bond had broken—he kept catching himself on those kinds of thoughts whenever he looked at Adam. It wasn't that he saw Adam in a different way. It was just... in addition to wanting to be held in Adam's arms, he also kept staring at those arms. He wanted to run his hands over those arms, slip his hands under Adam's clothes and feel him up everywhere, feel his warm skin and hard muscles.

"Yes," Adam said, his voice quiet but firm. "I know how it looks, but you don't know Harry. I do."

Jake raised his eyebrows. "Do you?" He huffed. "For fuck's sake, Adam! I don't get how you can be so blind about him! That little prick has been lying to you for ages, he disappears without warning and then reappears months later without explanation and you take him back? Just like that? Is he that good at sucking your cock?"

A muscle jumped in Adam's clenched jaw. He leaned to Jake and gritted out something too quietly for Harry to hear.

Harry looked down, trying not to be offended by Jake's accusations. He understood why Jake was angry. From Jake's point of view, Harry looked... not good.

But he didn't like that Jake was making Adam feel bad and angry.

"If you have a problem with me, you should talk about it to me," Harry said amicably. "I'm here, you know."

Jake turned to him with a scowl. "Look, don't get me wrong," he said. "I had nothing against you. But then you pulled a disappearing act, and my best friend was a right miserable asshole while you were gone—"

"Jake," Adam said, a warning in his tone.

"Fine," Jake said, lifting his hands with a huff. "I'm shutting up. But don't you have a fiancée or something?"

"I..." Harry said. "It's complicated."

"Unbelievable," Jake said, shaking his head. "Whatever." He looked at Adam. "Don't tell me I didn't warn you when he fucks you over again."

He left Adam's office, muttering something angrily under his breath.

Silence fell over the room.

Harry looked at Adam hesitantly. He didn't like the expression on his face.

"The thing is," Adam said with a humorless smile. "Jake is right."

Harry stomach dropped.

Adam walked over to Harry, the look on his face almost grim. Putting his hands on the desk on either side of Harry, Adam looked at him intently.

"You're going to fuck me over," he said, his tone very mild, contradicting the grim, unsmiling look in his eyes. "Aren't you, babe?"

Harry swallowed, licking his lips.

Adam leaned in and pressed his nose against Harry's cheek, nuzzling into him. "Yes, you will."

He shook his head dazedly.

"You will," Adam said again, dropping a barely there kiss on the corner of Harry's mouth. Harry made a small sound and parted his lips eagerly, chasing Adam's mouth with his.

"Fuck," Adam said, cradling Harry's face in his hands. He kissed the other corner of Harry's mouth. "How are you so fucking... It's like you were created to fuck me up. You've been lying to me—you're still lying to me, but a part of me doesn't give a shit. And it pisses me off." He finally kissed Harry for real, his lips greedy but soft.

Harry kissed back, hungry, so hungry, wanting to swallow Adam, wanting to have him, take him inside himself and never let him out. He wanted to be kissed harder, deeper, forever. He wanted so much. Until Adam, he'd never known it was possible to want a person so much, to crave them, to want to be physically joined with them. He was so hard already, hard and aching. He wanted—wanted—he wanted Adam to shove him on the desk, fill him up and make them whole.

Adam groaned and broke the kiss, leaning his forehead against Harry's. "Not here," he said tersely before diving for another kiss.

All too soon for Harry's liking, Adam pulled back again. Whining, Harry tried to bring their mouths back together.

Adam laughed hoarsely and practically jumped away from him. "Dammit, Haz," he said, his breathing unsteady, his cheeks flushed and dark eyes glassy. He loosened his tie and averted his gaze. "Don't look at me like that."

"Like what?" Harry said, rubbing at his swollen, oversensitive lips.

"Like you want me to fuck you on my desk."

"But I do." Harry crossed his legs tightly and put a hand on the bulge in his jeans, trying to relieve the ache.

Adam groaned, raking his hand through his hair. "Don't say that," he said. He looked pained. "How am I supposed to work when you look at me this way?"

"I can go," Harry offered, even though it was the last thing he wanted. He didn't want to be away from Adam. He stared at Adam longingly. He wished they could be joined physically all the time—he wished he could feel Adam in his mind.

"I don't want to get you in trouble," Harry said when Adam said nothing. "I can go."

Adam pinched the bridge of his nose and sighed. "Yeah, it's probably better if you do. I can't focus on anything with you here. Go before I get fired. We can meet during my lunch break."

"Okay," Harry said, hopping off Adam's desk. "I'll wait for you at the coffee shop."

Adam nodded briskly.

Neither of them moved. They stared at each other.

Adam chuckled and turned away. "Fuck, this is ridiculous. Get out. Now."

Harry left, smiling to himself.

In the corridor, he stopped and then ran back inside to kiss Adam one more time. Just one.

He left twenty minutes later, feeling thoroughly kissed, giddy, and loved up.

Harry chuckled, pressing his fingers to his swollen, oversensitive lips.

They really were being ridiculous. It was just a few hours.

What could possibly happen in a few hours?

Chapter 20

Time positively dragged when you waited for something, Harry noted, sighing to himself.

"Something wrong with your coffee, Haz?"

Harry glanced at his untouched coffee before shaking his head. "It's fine," he said, smiling at Samantha. She had been really angry at him when she had first seen him ("How could you just disappear like this? I was worried, you prat!"), but thankfully she had forgiven him.

"I'm just..." Harry squirmed when she shot him a knowing look.

"Oh my god," she said, grinning. "You finally fucked him."

The bell chimed.

"I—" Harry said before noticing that Samantha's eyes were elsewhere.

"Holy shit," she murmured, looking at something behind Harry. "Look at that hottie, Haz."

Curious, Harry turned—

And froze.

A tall, broad-shouldered man stood by the entrance, sweeping a cool gaze of silver eyes around the coffee shop. His long midnight-blue hair was tied back and did nothing to soften the razor-sharp cut of his firm jaw or the steel in his gaze as his pale eyes locked with Harry's.

Harry tried to make himself smaller.

"He's looking at you, Harry!" Samantha whispered excitedly. "How are you so lucky? First Adam and now—"

"He's my brother," Harry said with a sigh, watching resignedly as Ksar made his way to him.

Ksar was angry.

He might look calm and collected, but Harry knew he was actually angry. It wasn't that he could get a read of Ksar's thoughts. He never could, and, to his surprise, Harry still couldn't penetrate Ksar's mental shields despite his much-improved telepathic abilities. Not that he was trying very hard. Technically, he would be committing a crime if he did.

But he knew Ksar. He didn't need to read his mind to be able to tell that his brother wasn't pleased with him. To put it mildly.

"Brother?!" Samantha exclaimed just as Ksar reached them.

"Harry," Ksar said carefully.

Harry thought it was the first time Ksar actually called him Harry. He wasn't surprised. Ksar might be a stickler for the rules back home, but as a Lord Chancellor of the Ministry of Intergalactic Affairs, he was well-versed in other planets' customs and would never do something that would betray that they weren't humans. Even the way he was dressed was impeccably human.

While Harry was hopeless at human fashion, Ksar was wearing an expensive-looking dark suit that wasn't all that different from the ones Adam wore.

At the thought of Adam, Harry panicked a little. Adam's lunch break was going to start soon. Adam could enter the coffee shop any minute now.

"Hi," Harry said, frantically trying to decide what to do. Introducing Adam to Ksar would be a terrible idea. But he couldn't just leave with Ksar. Harry had promised to wait for Adam. Not to mention that Harry was scared that if he left with Ksar, he would never see Adam again. He wouldn't put it past Ksar to teleport him home as soon as they were out of humans' sight.

Samantha cleared her throat pointedly and Harry finally remembered his manners.

"This is Samantha, my former coworker," he said, gesticulating between her and Ksar. "My brother, Ksar."

Crap. Should he have invented a more human name for Ksar? Did Ksar sound human enough?

Ksar shot him an unimpressed look but nodded politely at Samantha. "Pleased to meet you," he murmured.

She blushed, touching her hair and looking at Ksar from under her eyelashes. "Pleasure is all mine," she said, her voice sounding a little weird.

For the first time Harry understood the meaning of secondhand embarrassment. He was no longer as clueless in such matters and could see that Samantha was attracted to Ksar. He wished he could tell her not to bother.

If Ksar noticed that she was flirting with him, he didn't show it, his eyes shifting back to Harry. "Where is he?"

"Who?" Harry squeaked.

Did Ksar know about Adam?

"Seyn," Ksar said, giving him a strange look.

Right.

Before Harry could answer, the doorbell chimed again, and a few customers entered the shop.

"Sorry, I have to get back to work," Samantha said with regret.

"I can help!" Harry said quickly, springing to his feet.

Except Ksar grabbed his wrist and sat him down.

"He can't," he told Samantha in a vaguely apologetic tone, not looking apologetic in the least.

As soon as she nodded and left them alone, Ksar said quietly, "Explain yourself, Harht."

Harry sagged in his seat in defeat. "How did you find me?"

Ksar gave him a flat look. "Did you really think I wouldn't?"

"But Seyn had our identification chips removed," Harry said. He did expect his family to find him eventually, but he didn't expect for it to happen so soon.

Something flickered in Ksar's eyes. He shrugged. "It wasn't hard to figure out you could be on Terra after you tried to convince Mother to let you go back. Besides, all our familial links to you were cut off again, making it obvious you're on a faraway planet." A disdainful sneer twisted Ksar's lips. "I'm not surprised Seyn lacked the foresight to see this, but I expected better from you. Is stupidity contagious?"

"Don't be mean," Harry said, frowning at his brother's cold, cutting tone. He never understood the open disdain Ksar had for Seyn. Ksar was usually so collected, but he was downright mean to Seyn.

"It's not kind to talk this way about your bondmate."

A sour look crossed Ksar's face at the unwelcome reminder that Seyn wasn't just Harry's best friend but also his bondmate.

For the first time, Harry fully understood why Seyn wanted to break his bond to Ksar so badly. Harry wouldn't want to be bonded for life to someone who despised him, either.

Not to mention there clearly was something faulty with Ksar and Seyn's bond, because it wasn't normal for bondmates to dislike each other. The bond usually prevented it. They must be really incompatible if even the bond couldn't make them fond of each other.

"Kind? I'm not kind, Harht," Ksar said with faint amusement in his voice. "You're the only one who's delusional about it."

"I'm not delusional," Harry said. "I know you pretend to be heartless, but deep down you care a lot."

Ksar just shook his head, looking at Harry like he was the silliest creature he'd ever seen but was still fond of against his better judgment. Which proved that Harry was totally right!

Right?

"I don't know how the hell you're related to our mother or me," Ksar said, his lips twisting. "You're like a chicken hatched in a nest of k'hlers."

"Now you're being mean to yourself and Mother," Harry said.

Sure, their mother and Ksar could be stern and ruthless, but they were nothing like k'hlers—the poisonous Calluvian predators similar to Terran snakes, only with wings.

"I'm being honest, not mean," Ksar murmured before boring his silver eyes into Harry's. "Why are you here? Why did you want to return to Earth?"

Harry licked his dry lips. Before he could say anything, the doorbell chimed again and Adam entered the shop.

Harry froze.

Adam smiled at him before his gaze flicked to Ksar, who still had his hand around Harry's wrist. Adam's smile disappeared, his shoulders visibly tensing.

He strode toward the table, his eyes still locked on Ksar's hand on Harry.

As if sensing something, Ksar turned around just as Adam reached them.

"Who is this, Harry?" Adam said, shouldering past Ksar and laying a hand on Harry's nape.

Both men exchanged a cold look over Harry, Adam's expression vaguely hostile and Ksar's vaguely suspicious.

Harry bit his lip, eyeing them warily. They were of similar height and build. Harry wasn't sure which of them would win if there was a physical altercation.

Tentatively, he extended his mental shields to Adam, protecting him from telepathic prying. Not that he thought Ksar would do it—it was a crime, after all—but he wouldn't put it past him. Ksar could be absolutely unethical if he thought it was necessary. Harry was aware his brother was a bit of a hypocrite in that regard. He insisted that everyone should follow the rules and laws, but he seemed to have no problem disregarding the rules if it suited him.

Harry hoped Ksar wouldn't try prying into Adam's mind.

If he did, he would find Harry's shield, which would make Ksar more than just suspicious. A Class 1 telepath shouldn't have been able to extend his mental shields to another person, and Harry was supposed to be Class 1.

"This is my brother, Ksar," Harry said.

Catching Ksar's incredulous look, Harry realized he had leaned back into Adam's touch. He hastily straightened.

"Brother?" Adam said.

"Ksandr," Ksar corrected curtly. "Alexander. And you are?"

Adam glanced at Harry before returning his dark eyes to Ksar. "Adam Crawford," he said, his tone still cold.

"He's my flatmate," Harry said quickly.

He felt Adam stiffen and winced on the inside. He had so much explaining to do.

"Flatmate," Ksar repeated, glancing at Adam's hand on Harry's neck. His face was completely inscrutable.

"Yes," Adam said in a clipped voice.

"London is expensive," Harry said, breaking the tense silence.

"I'm sure it is," Ksar murmured before smiling nicely. It was a little unnerving. Ksar rarely smiled nicely without a reason. "But I'm here now and you don't have to worry about it anymore. I'll take care of it."

Harry felt Adam's irritation spike. Before he could say anything, Ksar said, looking at Harry, "Mother is eager for your return. Let's get Seyn and leave."

Adam sucked a breath in.

Harry grabbed Adam's hand and didn't move from his chair.

"Harry," Ksar said, his pale eyes boring into him.

Harry took a deep breath, looked at Adam's grim face, and shook his head. "I'm not going," he said, looking at Adam.

The tension in Adam's jaw decreased a little.

"Pardon?" Ksar said testily.

Harry got to his feet and looked at Ksar. He nearly flinched at the expression on his brother's face. "I want to stay," he said haltingly, taking a step toward Adam until his back was pressed against Adam's chest. He calmed considerably as soon as Adam put a hand on his hip, anchoring him.

"I want to stay here," he said, firmer this time.

Ksar stared at him before his gaze slowly dropped to Adam's hand on Harry's hip. Harry felt himself flush. If Ksar had any doubts about the nature of his relationship with Adam, they must be gone now for sure.

And then Harry felt it—a heavy telepathic touch that undid all his mental shields in a matter of seconds. He'd never felt something like that and could only stare at Ksar. It wasn't just an immense breach of privacy; it should have been impossible. Harry was at least a Class 3 telepath now that his bond was gone. All modern Calluvians were supposedly no stronger than Class 2. Ksar shouldn't have been able to do this. It should have been impossible.

"Where's your bond?" Ksar's voice sounded in his mind, cold and harsh.

Harry shook his head dazedly. He didn't understand. How had Ksar done this? Ksar was bonded. His telepathy shouldn't have been so strong.

"Answer me, Harht."

Harry flinched, a headache splitting his head. *"Stop, it hurts,"* he thought at Ksar.

Immediately, the pressure receded, but Ksar continued glaring at him.

"I'll explain later," Harry told Ksar telepathically. *"I promise."*

"Not later. Now. Get rid of the human or I'm dragging you out of here by force."

Harry gave Ksar a pleading look, but his brother was unmoved.

Sighing, Harry turned to Adam. "I have to go back to your flat with my brother," he said, looking down at their tangled fingers. Adam's fingers were so much darker than his. They looked almost brown against his fair skin. His hand also dwarfed Harry's. It made Harry feel strange. He wanted to hide his hand inside Adam's. He wanted to hide himself under Adam's skin and stay there forever. "He wants to see Seyn. They're engaged," he clarified in case Adam had forgotten, playing with Adam's fingers.

"Harry," Adam said.

Biting his bottom lip, Harry lifted his eyes to Adam's. Adam's face was oddly still and blank. "You're not leaving," he stated. "Are you?"

Ksar cleared his throat behind Harry, impatient.

Harry ignored him, his gaze locked with Adam's.

He wanted to tell Adam he wasn't going anywhere, that he would be waiting for him when Adam returned home this evening.

But... could he give such a promise?

By the Calluvian law, he wasn't free to do as he wished. He wouldn't be allowed to stay on a planet like Earth. Pre-TNIT planets were off-limits for living, and only occasional visits were allowed.

The law prohibited interfering with the development of young civilizations or sharing superior knowledge and technology with them.

Harry understood why the law was necessary. Before the law had been introduced, there had been many catastrophic precedents in the past, with societies unable to handle technological advantages wisely. So yes, Harry did understand.

It didn't mean he was okay with it.

"I," Harry said. "I..." He searched for something to say, for something to reassure Adam—both of them—that it wasn't the last time they were seeing each other.

But he glanced at Ksar's stony face and couldn't think of anything that would make it possible for him to stay on Earth. Ksar might love him, but Harry didn't have much hope for convincing his brother to help him. Ksar would never understand. Ksar would likely grab him and Seyn and return them home where mind adepts would restore Harry's bond to Leylen'shni'gul.

Basically, it was hopeless.

"I," Harry croaked, his throat thick with some awful emotion he couldn't quite name as he looked into Adam's dark eyes.

"Harry, enough," Ksar said, his tone steely. "Let's go."

Harry swallowed, looking at Ksar's impatient, unimpressed face.

He looked back at Adam, his vision swimming. Panic rose swiftly, threatening to choke him. He couldn't breathe.

He couldn't breathe.

"Baby," Adam said, his grim expression shifting into one of concern. "Are you okay?"

A high sound tore out of Harry's throat and he crashed his face into Adam's chest, clinging to him with all his might, silent tears streaking his cheeks and wetting Adam's shirt. He couldn't breathe.

Distantly, he could hear Ksar's voice, but it was like white noise. All he could hear was Adam's low, soothing voice, whispering endearments into his ear as Adam's hands stroked his back, trying to calm him down.

Harry tried to calm down but couldn't, because—because he finally truly realized this was the last time Adam was holding him, the last time he would hear Adam's voice, the last time he would breathe in Adam's scent or feel the strength of Adam's body around him, against him.

He was hit with another wave of crushing panic, and he clung harder to Adam, never wanting to let go.

It took Harry a while to realize he was muttering something. "I don't wanna go, don't make me, I need you—don't make me go—I need you—"

"Harht," Ksar's voice filled his head. *"Cease this immediately. You're speaking in Calluvian."*

Harry shut his mouth but couldn't calm down no matter how hard he tried. His heart beat fast in his chest, his fingers clenched in Adam's shirt, unwilling to let go. He wasn't letting go. He wasn't. He would never.

"Babe," Adam said, threading his fingers through Harry's hair. "Look at me. Please. Come on, show me your pretty eyes."

Harry let Adam lift his face from Adam's chest. He could barely see Adam through the blur of tears, so it took him a few moments to realize Adam was staring at him oddly.

"Harry," he said. "Your tears are pink."

Harry blinked, trying to understand why it was significant. Behind him, he heard Ksar sigh.

"Human tears are colorless, Harht," Ksar's voice sounded in his head. *"Good job. Good luck explaining it."*

But Harry couldn't bring himself to care. He could feel nothing but the crushing, aching longing and the sense of impending loss.

"What in the world…" Adam murmured, bewilderment all over his face as he touched Harry's cheek to wipe his tears. "Are you bleeding somewhere?"

Harry turned his head to kiss his fingers.

"Harht," Ksar's voice snapped in his mind.

Harry ignored him, nuzzling into Adam's hand.

"Harry," Adam said, but he wasn't pulling away, brushing his hand over Harry's cheek, letting Harry nuzzle into it.

Harry lifted his eyes to meet Adam's confused dark ones, and then he whispered, "I love you."

Adam sucked a breath in. Harry heard Ksar make a sharp noise, too, but his eyes remained on Adam.

The longer Adam stayed silent, the more Harry's chest hurt.

"Haz, you can't just—I need a fucking explanation for once—oh, fuck it—" Adam dove in and kissed him, his mouth hungry and wet and so perfect. "Me, too, babe," he muttered against Harry's mouth. "I love you."

Harry melted into the kiss, his body doing that ridiculous thing where it tried to mold itself into Adam's. Everything else disappeared, there was only Adam everywhere, and not enough of Adam—

He was yanked away from Adam.

Opening his eyes, Harry found himself looking at Ksar's stony face. "We're leaving," Ksar said, very evenly.

Harry flinched. A seemingly calm Ksar was much worse than an angry one.

Before he could say anything, Ksar dragged him toward the exit.

Harry looked back at Adam, expecting him to stop them, but Adam didn't, standing very still. There was something very odd about him: his gaze was unfocused and confused, as if he had no idea what was happening or where he was. He didn't even glance Harry's way, rubbing at his temples with a pinched look on his face.

With dawning horror, Harry realized Ksar had done something to him.

"What did you do to him?" Harry said, trying to free himself from Ksar's grip. "What did you do?"

Ksar didn't answer, his face hard as he dragged him toward a cab. He pushed Harry inside and told the driver Adam's address in a stiff voice.

"How do you know Adam's address?" Harry said, looking back at the coffee shop. "Let me go back! Please, Ksar."

The driver looked uncertainly between them. "Drive," Ksar said, and of course his air of authority made the driver obey.

Harry opened his mouth to ask more questions, demand Ksar to return him to Adam, but the look Ksar leveled him with made him close it. Ksar gave off so much anger and disapproval it turned Harry's stomach.

Harry folded his hands on his lap and turned away, anger and resentment burning his insides. He didn't know how to deal with them.

He'd never felt such anger, especially toward his own brother.

But there was another emotion stronger even than his anger: the feeling of crushing loss.

He felt like he'd left a part of himself back in the coffee shop.

A part of him he'd never get back.

Chapter 21

As soon as they arrived, Ksar got out of the car and said coldly, "I hope you don't expect me to drag you like a child again. Walk."

Harry walked, glaring at Ksar's back but not daring to speak. For the first time ever, he understood why people's attitude toward Ksar ranged from wary dislike to fear.

Seyn opened the door with a smile that disappeared as soon as he saw Ksar. He paled and then promptly flushed.

"I'm not going," was the first thing Seyn said, a mulish expression appearing on his face.

"I'll deal with you later." Ksar shouldered past him into the flat with a terse, "Close the door, Harht."

Harry shut the door and crossed his arms over his chest. "I'm not going, either."

Ksar turned around, leveling them both with such a murderous look that it made Harry take a step closer to Seyn. He had to remind himself that this was his brother, not a stranger.

But try as he might, he couldn't forget the force of Ksar's telepathy, the things Ksar could do that he shouldn't have been able to do. Maybe Ksar was a stranger after all.

"You know what?" Seyn said, flipping his silver locks over his shoulder. "I refuse to be treated like a guilty child. If you have something to say, quit trying to intimidate us and just say it."

"If you don't want to be treated like a child, stop behaving like one," Ksar said, a sneer twisting his lips for a moment as he looked at Seyn before looking at Harry. "Explain yourself."

Harry glared. "Why? You already know everything. You saw everything in my mind—without asking permission."

"What?" Seyn said, whipping his head to stare at Harry. "He—but how?"

Of course Seyn was confused. Seyn knew how much stronger Harry's telepathy had become. Harry wished he knew the answer to Seyn's question.

Ksar unbuttoned his jacket and threw it on the couch. "I didn't see everything," he said. "I was too startled by the fact that my supposedly bonded brother engaged in sexual intercourse with a member of a pre-TNIT civilization."

Harry flushed. "You had no right to pry into my mind like that. You broke the law!"

"I think the Council would excuse me in this case," Ksar said. "I wouldn't have broken into your mind if you didn't behave like a wanton with that human. What happened to your bond?"

"My bond broke toward the end of my last stay on Earth," Harry said. "I don't want it back. My senses are so much better without it."

Ksar gave him a flat look. "I'm sure that's the reason you don't want your bond back."

Harry pursed his lips. "My telepathy has never been stronger."

"Yes," Ksar said, his tone very dry. "I saw how you used it to get to this city."

"You hypocrite," Seyn said when Harry had looked away guiltily. "You have no right to judge Harry for that when you violated his privacy in the worst possible way." His green eyes narrowed. "By the way, how is it possible? Harry is at least Class 3 now. You're supposedly Class 2. Supposedly."

"I haven't given you leave to speak," Ksar said, throwing a cold look Seyn's way. "Stay out of it. This is a family matter."

Seyn smiled at him sweetly and blew him a kiss. "But I'm practically family, aren't I?"

A muscle twitched in Ksar's jaw. "Not yet."

"Not ever," Seyn corrected him. "If you pried into Harry's memories, you know why I came to Earth. I want to get rid of the bond, too."

Ksar's face betrayed absolutely no emotion. "I have more important matters to deal with right now than your spoiled tantrums. Go to another room and wait until I'm finished with Harht."

Seyn flushed. "You—you can't just—you can't treat me like that!" He straightened to his full height and glared at Ksar. "I'm Prince Seyn'ngh'veighli of the Third Grand Clan, not your goddamn slave."

"Then act like it," Ksar said before looking at Harry sharply. "Stop worrying about the human. He'll be fine. I simply removed his memory of your little break down."

Harry pressed his lips together. "I don't believe you," he said. "Swear to me you didn't erase his memories of me," he said, voicing the fear that had been plaguing him since Adam hadn't even glanced his way when they'd left the coffee shop.

Ksar was quiet for a few moments, his face hard to read.

"I didn't, but it would have been for the best, wouldn't it?" he said at last. "It's better for everyone involved if he doesn't remember you. He'll never see you again."

Harry felt his eyes burn, a thick lump forming in his throat. He looked at Ksar pleadingly.

Ksar's expression remained stony. "Get your things, both of you. Leave nothing behind. You're not coming back. We're leaving."

Harry's chest hurt. Hurt and ached, as if someone had twisted his heart in their hands like a rag to wring all the blood from it.

Seyn made a sympathetic sound and put an arm around Harry's shoulders, glowering at Ksar. "How can you be so fucking heartless to your own brother? You bastard!"

Ksar's lips twisted into a derisive smile. "If I didn't know better, I would think you were a low-bred son of a Sarvakhu whore, not a scion of kings. Mind your foul tongue, kid."

Seyn scowled. "Don't you call me kid!"

"What should I call a spoiled child?"

Harry stopped listening. Instead, he stared at his brother's stony face and realized there was no changing his mind.

Ksar had made up his mind. Harry was never coming back. He was never coming back.

He was never going to see Adam again.

"I love him," Harry whispered. "Doesn't that matter?"

Ksar and Seyn stopped arguing and turned their heads to him.

Seyn sighed. "I'm so sorry, Harry."

But Harry didn't look at him. He looked at his brother's expressionless face. "Don't my feelings matter?" Harry hated how his voice broke on the last word, but it was hard to swallow that his big brother—the one who had taught him how to ride zhylk'ki and comforted him every time Harry had fallen, the one who had let him follow him around like a puppy when Harry had been a child—that Ksar didn't care about his happiness. It hurt. It hurt in a different way than the hurt he felt at the thought of never seeing Adam again.

Ksar's expression changed, just a little. "You don't love him," he said testily. "What you feel is infatuation. You aren't used to the lack of bond. Everything is new for you. You have too many feelings you don't know how to handle. It will pass."

Harry shook his head. "I need him," he said, looking Ksar in the eye. "I need him with my mind, with my heart, and with my body."

Beside him, Seyn choked, but Harry didn't blush. This was too important for him to be embarrassed.

Ksar's jaw clenched. He looked distinctly uncomfortable, as if he didn't expect Harry to be so straightforward and shameless.

"You're confusing lust with love," Ksar said. "You're too young and inexperienced to know the difference."

"Wait," Seyn cut in sharply. "What is that supposed to mean? How do *you* know the difference?"

"That's none of your concern." Ksar didn't look at him, his silver eyes still on Harry. "Do you think he loves you, Harht?" he said. "I saw his mind."

Harry fish-mouthed. Did Adam not love him back?

"He is rather besotted with you," Ksar admitted, rather reluctantly. "But the person he's besotted with is a cute, quirky human he met at a coffee shop, not a freaky telepathic alien." The look Ksar gave him was almost pitying. "You underestimate how much the truth would change his feelings for you."

"You don't know that," Seyn said.

"I do," Ksar said, still looking at Harry. "I've witnessed quite a few Contacts with secluded civilizations like Terrans. Most of the time they go horribly bad. Xenophobia aside, non-telepathic races tend to be very distrustful of telepaths. They don't like aliens who can mess with their minds and make them do their bidding."

"I'm sure the fact that you messed with Adam's mind wouldn't help now," Seyn said snidely.

"No, it wouldn't," Ksar said. "So even if I let you tell him, his reaction would crush you, Harht. I don't want you to be hurt."

"You're already hurting me," Harry said quietly.

Even if Ksar was right—even if Adam's reaction to the truth would be awful—it couldn't be worse than this horrible feeling of loss and guilt twisting his insides. He wanted Adam. Wanted to see him, lean against him and hide in his strong arms. Wanted Adam to kiss him behind his ear, call him his babe, and tell him that everything would be fine, that Adam got him.

If worse came to worst, Harry wanted the chance to explain everything and say goodbye. Adam deserved it. Adam deserved an explanation.

"Please," Harry said, looking Ksar in the eye and opening his mind to him, letting Ksar *see*.

Grimacing, Ksar broke the eye contact and said, "This conversation is pointless. You can't remain unbonded. We need to restore your bond to Leylen'shni'gul as soon as possible."

"Why?"

Ksar sighed, a troubled expression crossing his face. "Your bondmate and her parents came to the palace soon after you left. They reported that Leylen'shni'gul stopped feeling you in her mind. She still has the bond, but it's faulty and weak now. I reassured them that it was simply due to the distance between you and her, but they're getting nervous and suspicious, especially since no one knows where you are. We need to restore your bond before they might report it to the Council."

"Why?" Harry said, glancing at Seyn, who was weirdly quiet now.

Seyn was watching Ksar with a strange look on his face.

"Because they can't find out your bond is broken," Ksar said. "What do you think will happen if they do?"

Harry crossed his arms over his chest. "I don't think they can arrest me for accidentally getting rid of my bond. And technically, they can't make me bond to Leylen'shni'gul again, because the Bonding Law concerns only young children."

Ksar ran a hand over his face, shaking his head. "Don't be naive. Of course they can."

He looked at Harry. "You still have a binding betrothal contract. Do you really think the Council will let you be? The sole potentially high-level telepath in their midst while their own telepathy is suppressed by the bond?"

Harry flopped down on the couch, frowning deeply. "I'm pretty sure I'll test as Class 3 at most. I'm not all that dangerous."

Ksar gave him a pinched look. "And you think they'll just take your word for it?" He chuckled. "Can you name many civilizations with registered telepaths higher than Class 3?"

Harry bit his lip.

He could see Ksar's point. He could think of only two races that were classified as Class 4 on the Standard Telepathic Test.

"Yorgebs and Tajickssu," Harry said.

"And do you really think there are just two races in the entire galaxy that have Class 4 telepaths? Or that there are no higher level telepaths anymore?"

"It's possible to fool the Ministry's test," Seyn said quietly before Harry could respond. "It probably gets easier to fool it the stronger the telepath is."

Ksar nodded briskly. "They'll never believe you that you're just Class 3. You'll be watched all the time, at the very least. A small misdemeanor will be used against you as an excuse to prosecute you or use you as a tool for their agenda."

"What agenda?" Harry said.

Something cold flicked in Ksar's eyes. "Certain members of the Council insist that the Ministry's test is inconclusive and that having a telepath in charge of a grand clan shouldn't be allowed, because it might lead to abuse of power and it's supposedly 'unfair' to the telepathically null members of the Council."

Harry's brows furrowed.

There had always been some tension between telepathic and telepathically null Calluvians, and Harry was aware that lately it had been worse, but surely it wouldn't happen?

"But most ruling members of the grand clans are telepaths."

Ksar gave him a flat look.

"The ruling members of the grand clans aren't the only people in the Council. Need I remind you that the royal houses have only twenty-four votes and the rest of the votes belong to elected members, most of whom are telepathically null?"

Right.

"And you think they'd use me to further their agenda?" Harry said.

"I don't think it," Ksar said. "I know they will. You already used your telepathy against humans. A case like this is the perfect excuse they've been looking for. That's why you can't remain unbonded, Harht."

Harry's heart sank.

If what Ksar was saying was true, he had no choice. He would never forgive himself if his mother lost the throne because of him.

"The t-nulls should have pushed for the repeal of the Bonding Law instead," Seyn grumbled. "One would think it's in their best interests. Instead of being constantly bitter that they have next to no telepathy, why don't they do something about it?"

Harry shook his head. "Because there's no guarantee that repealing the Bonding Law would make things better for them. They must be scared that telepaths would become even more powerful if their bonds were removed."

"Yes," Ksar said. "Some believe that without the bond people who are now telepathically null would become just Class 1 telepaths, but the telepaths would become... something far worse."

Harry winced. In a way, he could understand why the telepathically null Calluvians were scared.

High-level telepaths could supposedly completely erase and replace a person's memory. They could make you believe your mother was a stranger. They could make you believe anything they wanted. No mental shields would protect you from them. They could damage or block areas of your brain, rendering you paralyzed or deaf. They could make you think you were being tortured. Class 7 telepaths could supposedly kill with their minds, shutting down your vital organs with as little as a thought.

It was understandable why the telepathically null members of the Council would be uncomfortable with the prospect of having such powerful telepaths in their midst. And Harry doubted that even the telepaths in the Council would support the repeal of the Bonding Law. Some of them would likely be tempted by the prospect of unlimited power, but if they repealed the law and broke all the bonds, where was the guarantee that they would be the powerful ones?

Repealing the law might completely overhaul the social hierarchy, which obviously wasn't in the Council's best interests. People in power never wanted change unless it benefited them.

The Bonding Law would never be repealed. And Harry would be considered a threat if the Council found out about his lack of bond.

Harry slumped back against the couch. "What options do I have? Besides going back and restoring my bond to Leylen'shni'gul?"

The look his brother gave him was almost sympathetic. "None."

"Bullshit," Seyn said.

Harry turned his head. "What?"

Seyn's gaze was fixed on Ksar. "You aren't bonded to me, are you?"

Harry frowned. What was Seyn talking about?

He looked at Ksar and found his expression carefully blank.

"I have no idea what you're talking about," Ksar said evenly.

Seyn laughed. "Do you think I'm stupid? When you described Leylen'shni'gul's symptoms, they sounded very familiar to me. I don't feel you on the bond's other end, and my bond is weak and faulty." He cocked his head to the side. "So, how high-level are you? Class 4? Class 5? Worse? Or should I say better? I guess now we know why you're such a high-handed ass."

A muscle started pulsing in Ksar's jaw.

Yet he didn't deny anything.

Harry stared at his brother. "Ksar? Is that true?"

Ksar swept a calculating gaze from Harry and Seyn.

"Don't even think of erasing our memories," Seyn said, tensing. "My mental shields are too intricate and personalized for you to rebuild them perfectly. I'll know they've been messed with and I'll go to mind adepts.

You wouldn't want them to find out what you did — or the state of my bond, for that matter."

Ksar's lips thinned, proving that he really had been considering erasing their memories. Harry couldn't believe him.

Seyn smiled humorlessly. "So you can go without a bond, but Harry can't, huh? Fucking hypocrite."

"It's different," Ksar said.

Seyn raised his eyebrows. "Enlighten us why it's different."

"Our bond never quite took," Ksar said, his voice slower, as if he was choosing his words carefully. "I'm not entirely sure why. Perhaps it was because of our age difference or the fact that I was much older than the age children got bonded at. Perhaps the painful death of my first bondmate damaged my ability to form a new bond. Either way, our bond has been defective from the beginning. You could never feel me through the bond, so you didn't know it wasn't normal. Leylen'shni'gul's bond to Harht had been perfectly functional, and she obviously can tell that something is wrong with the bond now. You could never tell the difference."

"So you used my obliviousness against me while all my life I wondered if there was something wrong with me." Seyn's voice wavered a little, but Harry didn't think Ksar noticed. Seyn chuckled. "Nice. And here I thought I couldn't dislike you more. Just out of curiosity, what were you going to do in two years' time? Fake the completion of the bond? Mess with my head and make me think our bond was fine?"

Ksar's face was awfully blank. Harry had a horrible suspicion that Seyn wasn't wrong.

"I haven't come to a decision yet," Ksar said. "But that was one of the options."

Seyn paled with fury.

Ignoring him, Ksar moved his gaze to Harry. "In any case, it's irrelevant for you. Leylen'shni'gul would definitely notice—she already has. And before you ask, she's not bonded to me, so I can't exactly 'mess with her head' and make her think her bond is fine, at least not indefinitely. It's not feasible."

Harry's shoulders slumped. Messing with Leylen'shni'gul's head would be a terrible thing to do anyway. Harry told himself he was glad it wasn't an option.

Ksar said, "If you don't come back, her parents will go to the Council. The consequences…you can't even imagine them. You have no choice, Harry."

Harry.

For some reason, the use of his human name by his brother hurt.

It finally made it real. He was going back. He had no choice.

Harry swallowed the hard lump in his throat, and said, "Just let me write him a note, then. I can't disappear without a word again. I can't do that to him, Ksar."

His brother studied him for a long moment before nodding. "Keep it brief. Don't say anything that'll get you into trouble. Hurry up. We're wasting time."

Harry turned and disappeared into Adam's bedroom. He grabbed a pen and a piece of paper from the drawer in Adam's room. He had to concentrate hard to make sure his handwriting was in English. The translating chip was a bit of a hit or miss when it came to writing.

It didn't help that his vision was blurry with tears and his hand was shaking as he wrote a short, inadequate message.

By the end of it, Harry could barely see the letters—or anything else, for that matter.

He dropped the paper on Adam's bed and wiped at his eyes.

Looking around the room, his gaze fell on the photograph of Adam with his arms around his parents. He was smiling widely, handsome and happy.

Harry's eyes welled with tears again.

Harry bit his wobbling lip before removing the picture from its frame, folding it carefully, and hiding it in his pocket.

"Are you ready, Harht? We're leaving," Ksar said from the doorway. Seyn stood beside him, a sullen expression on his face, his wrist firmly gripped in Ksar's hand.

"Take my hand," Ksar ordered, offering Harry his other hand.

Harry stared at it.

He looked around the room for the last time, at the note on the bed, and took a step toward his brother.

If Ksar noticed that his eyes were wet, he didn't comment on it as their hands clasped and the world—Earth—faded away, taking them away.

This time for good.

Chapter 22

Adam knocked on the door impatiently. When there was no answer, he told himself to get a grip. There was no reason to be anxious.

But no matter what he told himself, the niggling feeling that had been bothering him the entire afternoon only increased. Adam blamed Harry's brother. The whole encounter had been off—kind of bizarre, actually. Adam couldn't remember why he let Harry leave with his brother when he had been determined not to. He could only remember Harry promising him that he'd wait for him at home. Harry had told him that.

Adam pulled out his keys and opened the door.

His fingers were steady. His stomach wasn't tied into hard knots. He had no reason to feel that way. Maybe Harry was in the shower. Maybe he had headphones on and couldn't hear his knocking.

Adam pushed the door open.

The living room was empty.

The kitchen was empty, too.

A sickening sense of deja vu made it hard to breathe.

"Harry?" he called out roughly, his chest growing tight when silence was the only answer.

He strode to Harry's old bedroom. It was empty.

His heart beating somewhere in his throat, Adam went to his room.

It was empty, too. There was no sign of Harry anywhere.

Adam's gaze fell on the piece of paper on the bed.

He stared at it for a few seconds before slowly crossing the room.

He picked it up.

The handwriting was shaky and irregular, the letters slanted to the left instead of to the right.

Dear Adam,

I'm sorry. I hope one day you can forgive me and, looking back, say you were happy to have met me. I know I am. You were the best thing that ever happened to me. I feel so lucky to have met you. I just wish... I wish a lot of things, but I suppose it doesn't matter. Please believe me when I say that never at any point did I lie to you about my feelings. You made me feel so very happy and loved.

Please don't be mad at me. Or be mad at me if that's what you need to feel better.

I love you. I love you so very much. I hope you live a long, happy life full of laughter and love. I hope that when you are an old man, you'll look back and remember the silly, weird boy you once loved with some fondness instead of anger. I know I will always remember you.

Be happy. Please.

Yours,
Harry

Chapter 23

Harry had wondered where Ksar would even find a mind adept willing to restore Harry's bond and keep his mouth shut, but that question was answered when Ksar did it himself as soon as they arrived home, with ease and skill that made Seyn scowl at Ksar suspiciously. The fact that Ksar hadn't even needed Leylen'shni'gul's presence to do it was certainly eyebrow-raising, but Harry didn't really feel like questioning his brother. He wandered away from Ksar and Seyn, leaving them to their argument.

Having the bond back felt... strange. It felt off, like an uncomfortable, tight shirt he'd worn for years and had been okay with because he hadn't known better. But now he did, and the sense of wrongness was maddening, like an itch he couldn't quite scratch.

Harry had half-hoped the bond would make him incapable of missing Adam, but now he realized how ridiculous it had been. He had started having feelings for Adam long before his bond to Leylen'shni'gul had broken.

It seemed it was entirely possible to feel romantic love without the ability to feel sexual attraction. Even with the bond blocking the parts of his brain responsible for attraction, Harry's love for Adam still wasn't at all like his love for his family. It was tinged with raw need and hollow longing for *something*, but it was like there was a disconnect between his brain and his body. It felt like the feeling of thirst that he couldn't satisfy because he no longer had a mouth to drink. It was immensely frustrating.

Harry hastily blocked Leylen'shni'gul out of his mind; otherwise she would guess that there was something wrong with him. He also didn't want her to sense the resentment he felt toward her. None of this was her fault. Harry knew that. He shouldn't take his frustration out on her. She didn't deserve it.

With that in mind, Harry even managed to smile at Leylen'shni'gul when he met her and her parents during the formal dinner that evening.

"I'm glad you're back," she said, smiling at him across the table.

Harry stared at her. She was beautiful and soft-spoken. They'd had an amicable relationship all their life. Comfortable—that was what they had been. Harry tried to imagine touching her and being intimate with her. He couldn't. In fact, he felt rather nauseous at the prospect.

Eventually, Harry gave up and focused on the food, barely registering the conversations around him.

He could barely hear them anyway.

For a moment, he wondered if there was something wrong with his hearing. Every sound seemed muffled and distant. But then, as he put a spoonful of soup in his mouth and barely tasted it, Harry remembered the reason:

The bond was suppressing all his senses, not just the ones responsible for his telepathy or his ability to feel arousal.

Harry sighed. That would take some getting used to.

* * *

The fatigue and apathy started one month after his return home. Harry had never been a sickly person, so his lack of appetite surprised him a little, but he figured it was inevitable since he could barely eat the bland food. He tried not to let anyone notice that he wasn't feeling all that well. He didn't want his family's scrutiny.

Harry still had no idea what his parents knew. They hadn't spoken to him in depth about his unsanctioned trip to Earth. To be fair, neither had Sanyash: his sister had just shaken her head and said she was glad he'd come to his senses.

But then again, Sanyash wasn't around much, since she lived with her husband on a research space colony a few light years away. His parents didn't have that excuse. Harry could sense his mother's disappointment and disapproval every time she looked at him, but she had said very little to him on the matter. His father had jokingly told him not to be a brat and warn them next time he decided to disappear.

The lack of punishment had surprised Harry, but he had shrugged it off. He still didn't know what Ksar had told their parents—and he didn't care much.

In fact, Harry found that it was difficult for him to care about much of anything. He felt apathetic. Numb. Everything seemed dull. The world was dull. The food was tasteless. The colors were colorless.

Rationally, Harry understood that it must have been the bond messing with his perceptions, but it did nothing to change how he felt. Rationally, he might have understood that he had lived with the bond for most of his life and had been just fine, but after learning how much better and sharper everything could be, it was hard to get used to the blandness of everything—of his life. The bond just felt *wrong*. He felt as if he was put together wrong, too.

Therefore, considering the general state of his mood these days, his fatigue and apathy didn't worry Harry. He was probably just acclimatizing. It would get better.

It had to.

* * *

Months passed. The feeling that he was put together wrong only increased, the vague longing turning into a full-blown *ache*. Something hurt deep inside him, twisting him into knots. His lack of appetite was impossible to hide now, and Harry couldn't quite summon enough energy to pretend that he was fine. He wasn't fine.

"I think I'm dying," Harry said one day when Seyn asked why Harry looked so pale and sickly.

Harry wondered if he had caught something on Earth and it was killing him slowly.

Seyn looked horrified to hear that, for some reason.

"What the hell is wrong with you?" he said, smacking Harry on the head. "How can you just say it like you don't care?"

Harry stared at him and realized with some surprise that he really didn't. He didn't care whether he lived or died. It was probably bad. Was it?

"I don't even recognize you anymore!" Seyn said, jumping to his feet. "You used to be the most positive person I've ever known, always so nauseatingly optimistic about life, and now you're—" He cut himself off, his green eyes narrowing. "Of course. Ksar must have fucked up when he restored your bond."

Before Harry could tell him that he was wrong and the bond was perfectly functional, Seyn stormed out of Harry's room.

Harry sighed and wondered whether he should go after him, but it would require too much energy, energy he could no longer summon.

He wasn't sure how much time had passed before the door opened again.

"Just look at him!" Seyn said. "It doesn't even look like he's moved from that couch since I left him in the morning! Can't you see it's not normal?"

Ksar followed him into the room with a decidedly unimpressed look on his face.

Harry was somewhat surprised Seyn had found Ksar at all. Harry had barely seen Ksar lately. Ksar was always busy, which was hardly surprising, considering his countless duties.

"You shouldn't have messed with his mind," Seyn said. "You're not a professional mind adept. No doubt you fucked it up and now he's all weird and sickly!"

"I didn't 'fuck' anything up, as you so eloquently put it," Ksar said, but then he frowned, looking at Harry. "Harht?"

It took Harry a few moments to realize he was being asked something. "What?" he said belatedly.

"See?" Seyn said.

Ksar's silver eyes narrowed. He studied Harry carefully.

"Borg'gorn, run a full medical scan on Prince Harht," Ksar said.

"The scan is initiated," the AI said.

Harry shrugged, feeling vaguely bothered that his opinion wasn't even asked, but deep down, he knew it was probably a good idea. Something must be wrong with him. Lately he felt like he'd been... fading out of existence.

"Well?" Ksar said, eyeing Harry intently as Seyn paced the room.

The palace AI replied, "Would you like to hear the results now, Your Highness?"

"As soon as Seyn'ngh'veighli leaves."

"I'm not going anywhere." Seyn walked over to Harry, sat next to him, and put an arm around his shoulders.

Harry tried not to cringe and shy away from the touch. Physical affection was uncharacteristic for Seyn—for their entire race—and yet recently Seyn had been touching him so often. It made Harry feel a little humiliated. He didn't want anyone's pity.

He didn't want anything.

He wanted everyone to leave him alone.

Harry winced, trying to shake off the moodiness. Seyn was right: this was so unlike him. He wasn't this moody, subdued person.

"You may proceed, Borg'gorn," Seyn said.

"I apologize, Your Highness, but I cannot take orders from you. Only the Crown Prince has clearance to access medical records of the members of the Second Grand Clan besides the Queen and the King-Consort."

Sighing, Harry rubbed at his face. "Let Seyn stay, Ksar. Borg'gorn, go ahead, tell me what's wrong with me."

"With your permission, Prince Ksar?" Borg'gorn said.

Ksar shot Seyn a displeased look but nodded. "Go ahead."

"There are no foreign viruses in the prince's system. He is suffering from severe malnutrition and depression."

"So I'm okay?" Harry interrupted the AI. He wasn't all that fond of the intrusive nature of the AI's scanners.

"I would not say so, Your Highness," the AI said. "The malnutrition and depression are merely symptoms of the problem, not the problem itself."

"What do you mean?" Ksar said.

The AI replied, his voice careful, "Judging by his brain activity and hormone levels, it appears Prince Harht'ngh'chaali's condition stems from the fact that he is a throwback."

Seyn stiffened against Harry.

Ksar's brows furrowed. "Pardon?"

Harry frowned, confused. Of course he'd known he was a throwback, but it had always been a useless fact rather than something relevant.

It wasn't well known that a small percentage of their race shared biological traits with the surl'kh'tu, their primitive ancestor that lived around a million years ago. The throwback gene first manifested after the same genetic experiments that caused telepathic mutations, but unlike telepathy, physiological changes could not be changed by bonding the person's telepathic core, so everyone just pretended the problem didn't exist. What being a throwback entailed wasn't something discussed in polite company, and for a reason. Harry knew about throwbacks so much only because he was one.

Biologically, throwbacks were quite different from modern Calluvians. The surl'kh'tu had been intersex, and although throwbacks weren't intersex, they retained the ability to produce natural lubrication when they were aroused. It had always been just an irrelevant little fact to Harry.

He still didn't understand what it had to do with anything.

"I fail to see how it's relevant to the subject at hand," Ksar said, as if reading Harry's thoughts. For all Harry knew, he could well be.

"Isn't it obvious?" Seyn murmured, his body very still against Harry. "It's been scientifically proven that the surl'kh'tu were very selective. They had a single mate throughout their life. Scientists think that's why they eventually went extinct—they were too selective. If their mate died, they didn't take another mate."

Harry's heart skipped a beat.

He blinked, his ears ringing as he stared at Seyn.

He didn't understand.

"Indeed," Borg'gorn said. "Moreover, it has been proven by the Rivixu Institute scientists that after the first act of mating, a surl'kh'tu's body produced a certain hormone that made them… physically need their mate."

The AI actually sounded awkward. "A most fascinating biological mechanism that ensured reproduction and survival. It has been theorized that this evolutionary trait was formed as a response to a rapidly growing population of the derv'kh'tu, a telepathic subspecies of archaic Calluvians, moving into their habitat. But it wasn't enough—as we all know, the derv'kh'tu eventually displaced the surl'kh'tu. It was thought that the surl'kh'tu were out-competed and became extinct before the derv'kh'tu evolved into modern Calluvians, but the existence of throwbacks suggests that the two subspecies interbred to some extent."

Harry shook his head, his mind reeling.

Borg'gorn's words didn't make sense. "But he wasn't—he's a Terran."

He couldn't even *say* Adam's name.

Borg'gorn said carefully, "I do not think it matters, Your Highness. Although there have not been precedents of crossbreeding between Terrans and Calluvians, crossbreeding should be within the realms of possibility."

Harry licked his lips, for a moment allowing himself to imagine children with Adam's smile and dark eyes. His chest hurt, because it would never happen.

"Surely you don't believe it has anything to do with Harht?" Ksar said sharply. "My brother isn't a surl'kh'tu. They're long extinct. He just happens to have a few common traits with them."

Borg'gorn said, "We know that the surl'kh'tu traits are not equally strong in all throwbacks. Some throwbacks are barely different from most Calluvians while others share unusually many traits with the surl'kh'tu. It is not impossible for His Highness to share that particular biological trait with your ancestors—"

"Nonsense," Ksar said. "The surl'kh'tu might have literally needed their mates, but there is no scientific proof that throwbacks share that trait with them. There have been no precedents."

Seyn scoffed. "Of course there have been no precedents. Unlike us, the surl'kh'tu actually chose their mates. Throwbacks never had the same opportunity, because the Bonding Law was introduced soon after the first throwbacks were documented."

"No one asked for your opinion," Ksar said.

Seyn flushed with fury and glared at him. "I hate you so much," he said with feeling. "Can't wait to be free of you."

For the first time since his return home, Harry remembered about the one-sided state of Seyn's bond to Ksar. Since Seyn hadn't told anyone about Ksar's telepathy, they must have come to some sort of agreement. Probably. Harry wasn't sure. He hadn't cared enough to ask, and *that* spread the feeling of cold dread through his body. If he didn't care even about his best friend and his brother's future, what did it say about the state of his mind?

"But Seyn is right," Harry said, trying to think. It was difficult. Thinking was difficult. It was so hard to focus. "What are the odds of being bonded to the person you would have chosen if you weren't bonded? Probably extremely slim."

"Maybe," Ksar conceded, not even glancing at Seyn. He looked at Harry. "Let's return to the subject at hand. Am I supposed to believe Harht can't live without that Terran?"

A searing ache burned Harry's insides at the mere mention of Adam. Harry struggled to focus on the conversation.

"As there are no precedents, I can only hypothesize," Borg'gorn said. "But Prince Harht's readings are most worrying. He may not necessarily die, but I do think his physical and mental health will keep deteriorating." A pause. "May I speak freely, Prince Ksar?"

Ksar gave a clipped nod.

"I was going to inform you this evening that I had concerns about Prince Harht's health. I have taken the liberty of observing the young prince since his return from Sol III. I have noticed that his concentration has been deteriorating at an alarming rate. Yesterday he spent six-point-three hours without moving, staring at nothing I could see. I had to say his name seven times to make him react. If the prince's awareness of his surroundings keeps deteriorating at this rate, it is very likely that he will eventually fall into a comatose state, perhaps with a very limited awareness of his surroundings. I recommend daily injections of the surl'kh'tu hormone suppressants to make him more alert and focused, but it cannot be a long-term solution. Eventually they will stop working."

Seyn squeezed Harry's shoulder, worry rolling off him in waves. Harry was more concerned by the fact that he didn't feel very concerned.

"And you're absolutely certain that the cause is the throwback gene?" Ksar said.

"There is always a margin for error, but I am ninety-nine-point-two percent certain," the AI replied. "Besides the aforementioned hormone in his system, there are significant changes in the young prince's herovixu, the area of the brain that is specific for throwbacks."

Ksar's lips folded into a thin line before his eyes fixed on Harry. "Talk to me, kid. Is it really that bad?"

Harry moistened his dry lips. "I—I don't know. I haven't even noticed that I zone out for hours. But I feel..." He struggled to explain it. "I feel like there's a hole in me that's sucking me in from the inside out."

Ksar's face was grim. "And that's because of him? The Terran?"

Harry flinched, curling into himself. He didn't want to talk about Adam. Even thinking about Adam *hurt*. He wasn't sure he could talk about Adam without breaking down and begging Ksar to let him go back to Earth. He couldn't be so selfish. He wouldn't be so selfish. He wouldn't ruin his family with his selfishness. It would be pointless anyway, because Ksar had been right: the Council and the Ministry would never let him live on Earth, and he couldn't—wouldn't—keep dicking Adam around when he couldn't stay on Earth permanently. It would be selfish. Adam deserved better. Adam deserved someone who could make him happy. Someone who could be honest with him.

So what was the point in talking about it?

"Does it matter?" Harry said, barely moving his lips.

Ksar's eyes narrowed. All it took was one look, and Harry's flimsy mental shields collapsed, allowing his brother in. Harry didn't resist. He didn't think he could even if he wanted to.

Finally, moments or hours later, Ksar left his mind.

Ksar's jaw was clenched, his expression vaguely sick. "Your mind is a mess. Some parts of it don't react to stimuli at all. Borg'gorn is right. Your mind is dying, Harht."

Harry stared at his brother blankly.

Seyn pulled Harry closer, projecting comfort and protectiveness. "You are going to do something to help him, right?" he said, looking at Ksar.

Harry shook his head. What could Ksar do? Ksar might have been the Crown Prince of their grand clan and the Lord Chancellor of their planet's branch of the Ministry, but he didn't have the power to protect him from the Council or the Ministry. No one did. The legal troubles aside, the scandal alone would destroy their family if other Calluvians found out about Adam.

"Don't worry about me," Harry said. "I won't disgrace our family."

Ksar closed his eyes for a moment. "Harht—"

"I know," Harry said, biting his lip to keep it from trembling. He was a little afraid of dying, after all, but he almost welcomed the fear. It was better than the dull apathy and hunger without a name.

"But can't we just smuggle him to Earth?" Seyn said. "Like I did?"

"And then what?" Ksar said coldly. "It's impossible to delete the teleporter's history. Sooner or later, Harht would be found, and the consequences would be much worse. And even if he wouldn't be found, he'd never be able to step foot on his home planet and see his family. Is that the sort of life you want for him? Do you think he would be happy to live like that, with all his familial links gone? Telepaths are not meant to live without telepathic communication for long stretches of time. He would be miserable."

Seyn's chin lifted. "At least he would be alive and sane. We must do something!"

Ksar went very still. "*We* won't do anything," he said testily. "*You* will go home and keep your mouth shut about everything you've heard.

"How can you be so heartless?" Seyn exclaimed, getting to his feet. "He's your brother!"

"Yes," Ksar said. "He's my brother, and this is a family issue. You're not family. Leave. You overstayed your welcome a long time ago."

Seyn flushed with fury and humiliation before storming out.

"Why are you always so nasty to him?" Harry murmured.

Ksar's face closed off. "That's irrelevant. We have more important things to discuss."

"What important things?" Harry said, looking down at his hands. What was there to discuss, really? He was dying or going to become a vegetable. Harry almost hoped he would die; that seemed to be the better option. He didn't want to be a burden to his family.

He would never see Adam again, anyway. He hadn't been able to say goodbye to him in person, and now he never would. Adam would never know that Harry was gone. Adam probably wouldn't care, anyway. Adam probably hated him. Of course Adam hated him. Adam had probably forgotten him already. Adam had probably fallen in love with someone else. Someone human. Someone normal. Someone who—

"Harht," Ksar said. "Breathe. Harry!"

The command in his brother's voice made him realize his lungs hurt. Harry opened his mouth and closed it. He breathed. He tried to.

Ksar's expression softened. In a few long strides, he was by Harry's side. And then his arms were around Harry.

Harry clung to his brother, his eyes squeezed shut. Ksar hadn't hugged him in years.

When Ksar pulled back, his expression was grim and hard. He tipped Harry's face up and looked him in the eye.

"I can't promise you that it will be easy, Harry," Ksar said. "It won't be. But I promise you that I will find a solution." Something cold and ugly flickered in his eyes. "By any means necessary."

Chapter 24

Ksar was more or less satisfied as he left the Queen's office. He was pleasantly surprised that he hadn't had to influence his parents' minds to make them more... open-minded about Harht's situation. It seemed he wasn't the only one in the family with a soft spot for their youngest member. Granted, the Queen hadn't been happy to hear the news, but all in all, it had gone smoother than Ksar had expected. Their parents' concern for Harht had outweighed their dismay by the situation. Harht was going to need their parents' unconditional support while Ksar solved the problem of Harry's bond to Leylen'shni'gul and the fact that legally Harry couldn't have a relationship with the human.

Ksar pressed his lips together. He still couldn't say he was happy with the fact that Harry literally needed his human.

Initially, he had been skeptical of Borg'gorn's assessment of the situation until he checked Harry's mind himself.

What he had seen in Harry's mind was beyond disturbing. Harry's mind had always been warm and bright, full of happy, if naive, thoughts. Now it was dull and gloomy, lifeless and devoid of any excitement. Harry's brain was confused and sluggish, his core pulsing with such raw *need* that it nearly made Ksar sick.

Harry was also in immense pain, but his brain didn't seem to work correctly for him to feel it fully. The bond around Harry's telepathic core didn't make matters better, messing with the already suffering mind and body. Ksar couldn't imagine constantly living with that kind of pain and unsatisfied need.

He didn't think Harry could last long without going insane or his brain finally shutting down.

So regardless of his own thoughts on the matter, he would have to get Harry what he needed: that human of his.

Ksar gritted his teeth and strode toward his office.

He was annoyed by the situation. Though, perhaps annoyance wasn't the correct word. Cold rage fit better. He wanted to kill that human. Harht was still a kid. It wasn't Harht's age that was the problem—Ksar had been on hundreds of planets and was well aware that the Calluvian age of majority was considered rather old by most races' standards. Harht was twenty-three, old enough to make his own decisions.

No, the problem wasn't Harht's age, per se; it was Harht's naivety and trustfulness. Harht had been too sheltered all his life. He hadn't even attended an off-planet school, as most Calluvian princes did. Their parents had always babied Harht too much and he had grown up disgustingly naive and *nice*.

Ksar hadn't had an opportunity to observe Adam Crawford for long, but he was familiar with the type: the handsome, confident type that fucked every attractive thing. Harht deserved better.

But it didn't matter now, did it?

Ksar pressed his hand against the scanner and the door to his office whooshed open.

"Borg'gorn, the information I requested," he said, seating himself behind his desk.

A hologram appeared in front of him.

The AI replied, "The data is not complete, but the initial research indicates that twenty-three percent of the Ministry's Lord Chancellors would like for the laws regarding pre-TNIT races to be softened. Forty-six percent do not have particularly strong feelings on the matter. Thirty-one percent firmly agree with the law."

Ksar hummed thoughtfully. Twenty-three percent was better than expected. He could work with that.

"Has the Queen-Consort of the Sixth Grand Clan accepted my invitation?"

"Yes, Your Highness. She'll be here shortly."

"Good." Ksar leaned back in his chair and closed his eyes. His mind raced with possibilities, considering and discarding them quickly.

He wished he didn't have to choose that route.

For a moment, he wondered again if it would have been easier to simply smuggle Harht to Earth as Seyn had suggested, but he dismissed the idea again. To do that, he would have had to completely subdue the teleporter technicians' wills, erasing their memories again and again each time they saw in the teleporter's history that Harht had teleported to Earth.

Even if it were feasible—which it wasn't, since Ksar was too busy—there was nothing he could have done to keep the technicians' bondmates out of their minds; they would have noticed immediately that something was amiss.

No, the political route was safer and less convoluted in the long run.

He'd made the right choice.

"The Queen-Consort of the Sixth Grand Clan is here, Your Highness," Borg'gorn said.

Ksar opened his eyes and straightened in his chair. "Let her in."

The door opened and Queen-Consort Zeyneb'shni'waari strode in confidently.

Ksar didn't stand up. It would be the polite thing to do, but it certainly wasn't required or expected of him. As the Crown Prince of the Second Grand Clan and the future king of his clan, Ksar's social standing was higher than Lady Zeyneb's and they both knew it. Lady Zeyneb was neither a friend nor an ally—yet—and any false courtesy would only make her suspicious. He couldn't appear too eager.

"Ksar'ngh'chaali," she said with a smile. "I was pleasantly surprised to receive your message, given that you declined to support my bill last time."

"Were you?" Ksar murmured, looking her in the eye. A quick look into her thoughts revealed nothing he hadn't expected: she was curious and eager to use this opportunity to further her political goals. She was also wary of him. She didn't trust him.

Good. She wasn't completely foolish. He didn't need foolish allies.

"It's actually the reason I requested this meeting," Ksar said. "I'm willing to reconsider my stance."

Zeyneb cocked her head to the side. "And what changed your mind?"

Ksar smiled.

She shifted, looking a little uneasy.

"Your adopted brother is the Lord Chancellor of Planet Kiwufhi," he said. "I have heard that he's going to propose a bill in the next session of the Ministry."

She frowned, looking confused but intrigued. Ksar knew she wasn't interested all that much in intergalactic politics.

"What kind of law?" she said.

"Repeal of the 156th Ministry law," Ksar said.

She stared at him. "I'm sure you must have heard wrong," she said slowly. "That would be political and social suicide. It would never pass."

"Just like the bill you want to propose in the Council," Ksar said amicably. "But politics can be so unpredictable. You never know."

Her eyes narrowed. She gave him a long, assessing look.

"Perhaps," she said at last. "Perhaps we should speak plainly to avoid confusion."

Ksar smiled and leaned back in his chair. "If your adopted brother proposes the bill I mentioned in the Ministry's next session, the Queen will support the bill you intend to propose in the next session of the Council."

Her nostrils flared. Ksar didn't need to read her mind to know that she was interested.

"Your mother the Queen is very influential," Lady Zeyneb said slowly.

"But even that won't be enough for the bill to pass. There are too many telepathically null cowards in the Council."

Ksar looked at her steadily. "Let me worry about it."

She studied him. She did seem a bit skeptical, but she knew better than to question him. That would give her plausible deniability if he were caught.

And she wanted the bill to pass too much. It was hardly a secret. Lady Zeyneb had been pushing for the amendment to the Bonding Law for years. Her motives were transparent: she was acting on behalf of her son, who was bonded to the former heir to the Fifth Grand Clan. The match had been perfectly eligible, except her son's bondmate had disappeared decades ago, presumably kidnapped by the rebels. However, nothing was confirmed. Although the lost prince's identification chip had been deactivated, the bond to Lady Zeyneb's son remained, suggesting that the lost prince was alive…somewhere.

In any case, Lady Zeyneb's son needed to get rid of the bond if he was to marry the King of Planet Zicur, whom he had met at the off-planet school he had studied at and who had been courting him for years, which was the source of endless gossip in the society. If the King of Zicur weren't such an eligible bachelor, the situation would have been far more scandalous, since technically Lady Zeyneb's son was bonded.

It was no wonder Lady Zeyneb wanted to break her son's bond to the absent prince and marry him off to his prestigious suitor.

Ksar would do the same.

So he waited patiently for her to accept his conditions. She would not refuse.

At last, Lady Zeyneb nodded and stood. "Very well. I will contact my brother. I'm looking forward to hearing good news from you."

"You will," Ksar said, getting to his feet out of politeness.

She smiled at him and left.

As the door slid shut after her, Ksar sat down. Closing his eyes, he reached with his mind toward the woman's. Since she was alone now and supposedly safe of any telepathic prying, her mental shields were down and her mind was an open book.

He seems too interested in repealing the 156th law. That's a weakness I can exploit. Perhaps I should demand more things from Ksar in exchange for my brother's support. Hmm.

If Ksar had any lingering doubts—not that he had any—over what he was about to do, they would have been gone now.

Carefully, he planted a thought deep in her mind. Nothing radical. Nothing she would notice or consider uncharacteristic for her. It was simply a suggestion that she should do as Ksar wanted for the time being and that she could always turn the situation against Ksar at some point in the future—a very remote future.

She didn't notice anything.

But then again, why would she when everyone knew it was impossible to plant thoughts without eye contact?

Ksar smiled.

Infinite power corrupts, a voice said scathingly in the back of his mind. A voice that sounded suspiciously like Seyn's.

Ksar frowned and checked his mental shields, but they were impenetrable as always. He had imagined it.

Or perhaps it was the voice of his conscience he'd thought he no longer had.

Pressing his lips together, Ksar discarded the thought. He had no time for this. He had a busy day ahead of him. More people in need of persuading.

Persuading was a good word. It could mean a number of things.

Ksar drummed his fingers on the armrest.

But first, he had a special meeting before he could return to the political negotiations.

"Borg'gorn, is Lady Leylen'shni'gul here already?"

"Yes, Your Highness."

Ksar schooled his face into an amicable expression as the door whooshed open again, admitting Harht's bondmate.

Ksar studied her.

She was pleasant to look at, pleasant in manner and appearance. Harht was lucky. She was definitely less of a bother than Seyn.

A flash of irritation at the thought of Seyn made it more difficult to put on a smile for the girl.

"Lady Leylen'shni'gul," he said. "Please, take a seat."

Blushing slightly, she did. "Your Highness. Is there a reason you requested my presence?"

"There is," Ksar said, dropping his gaze.

For a moment, he considered simply forcing her to do his bidding, but he dismissed the idea.

It would be too risky.

A skilled mind adept could discover that she was being influenced—and if everything went as he planned, a skilled mind adept was going to examine her mind for a very specific reason.

"I'm afraid I don't have much time, so I'll speak candidly," Ksar said, softening his voice. "In a few months, an amendment to the Bonding Law will be passed. From then on, anyone who has reached the age of majority would be able to request the dissolution of their bond. You reach the age of majority in three months."

She stared at him. He could practically see her mind working. She wasn't a stupid girl. "You want me to request the dissolution of my bond to your brother?" she said slowly. "Why would I do that? I'm perfectly content with my bond."

Of course she was. While she was of noble blood, and her family owned one of the biggest deposits of *korviu*, the invaluable chemical element necessary for the use of transgalactic teleporters, her family's social standing wasn't very high. A prince was a catch for her. She would never willingly dissolve the bond to Harht.

Not for the first time, Ksar wished he could simply break Harht's bond to the girl himself—he was more than capable of it—but it wouldn't solve Harht's problem. It wouldn't make him free in the eyes of the law.

Ksar also wished he could simply wait until Harht reached the age of majority and could request the dissolution of the bond himself, but after seeing the state of his brother's mind, he didn't think Harht had that much time. Of course Ksar could have pushed for a complete repeal of the Bonding Law, but the Council would never vote for it, and it would be highly suspicious if everyone *suddenly* changed their mind.

So negotiating with Leylen'shni'gul was the only option. Luckily, Ksar knew something she would be more than willing to break her bond for.

Ksar met the girl's eyes. "And what if I offered myself in my brother's place?"

Her eyes widened. She blushed. "I... I'm afraid I don't understand, Your Highness. I thought you were bonded to Prince Seyn'ngh'veighli."

Suppressing another surge of annoyance, Ksar forced a pleasant look on his face. "Soon, I won't be."

She smiled.

Chapter 25

Calluvia didn't have winters. It didn't have deserts or wastelands. The weather was perfect most of the year. The surface was green and lush, ridiculously tall trees everywhere.

Harry had always loved this about his home planet, but now he couldn't help but notice how artificial it was. All of this was genetically engineered from the remains of extinct plants, and millions of agricultural robots looked after it. The planet looked vibrant and perfect on the surface, but it wasn't natural.

Harry wondered what Calluvia would look like if his people didn't interfere with the natural order of things. The lovely gevishku tree he was sitting under had been extinct for a million years before the geneticists decided to bring it back just because it was so pretty. Was it right?

Similarly, the throwback gene he was carrying would have never existed if the geneticists hadn't interfered with the natural order of things. The surl'kh'tu were long extinct, but here he was, a throwback to ancient times.

Harry leaned his cheek against the tree's smooth trunk and closed his eyes. He wondered if the tree was empty on the inside, too. Was it lonely, because it didn't really belong here? Could it feel pain? Or was it just numb by now?

"…Harry!"

Harry flinched and looked up.

His father was frowning at him, a look of great concern in his eyes, which made Harry wonder how long his father had been trying to get his attention. It had been happening a lot lately. Too often.

A shiver ran up Harry's spine. Was he going to disappear into his head one day and never come back? He hoped it wouldn't end that way. He didn't want to be some kind of vegetable. A death would be preferable.

To his relief, his father didn't comment on his lack of reaction. He sat next to Harry on the bench and looked at the fountain opposite them.

They sat in silence for a while.

"You were a surprise to us," his father said at last, his voice quiet and contemplative. "When your mother found out she was pregnant, she didn't want you. She argued that we already had the heir, and Sanyash was the spare. She insisted that she had no time for another child." His father smiled. "But I knew her. She was simply thrown off her balance. You know your mother likes to calculate her actions ahead of time. Ksar and Sanyash's births had been meticulously planned. She had specifically chosen the main traits she wanted them to have—leadership, superior intelligence, strong will—and their fetal development was supervised by the best geneticists at the Reproduction Center."

His father smiled at Harry. "You were very much unplanned, her only natural child, the only one she carried under her heart for ten long months. You're different from your siblings. You may not have their leadership qualities, but you have a good, kind heart."

Harry swallowed. "Why are you telling me this?"

His father squeezed Harry's shoulder. "There's no need to hide in the gardens, Harry. Your mother may not show it, but she loves you more than any of her other children. She may not approve of your choices and may not be happy about the…situation, but all she wants is for you to be healthy and happy. You're her baby and always will be. I'm pretty sure she won't disown you even if you murder someone." His father chuckled. "Don't tell her I told you that. She always says we spoil you too much as it is."

Harry smiled back shakily and hid his face in his father's shoulder. "Thank you," he said hoarsely. "I love you, Father."

His father patted him on his head. "I love you too, kid. Just hold on. Your brother is working on a solution as we speak." He chuckled. "I suppose we must be glad now that Ksar was created to succeed, no matter how impossible it might seem."

* * *

Calluvian Political Herald
Intergalactic Union Date: 18768.038

...There are strong rumors of intense lobbying happening in the Council. If the rumors are to be believed, Lady Zeyneb'shni'waari, the Queen-Consort of the Sixth Grand Clan, is going to propose a bill with amendments to the Bonding Law. It is not the first time she expressed such ambitions, but if the rumors are any indication, this time the bill has a chance to pass.

Calluvian Political Herald
Intergalactic Union Date: 18768.108

Breaking! A repeal of the 156th law has been proposed at the Ministry's 2311th session.

The 156th Ministry law, colloquially known as "Pre-TNIT law," is the law concerning civilizations that have not reached the technological level required for Contact. Currently the law forbids the Union of Planets' citizens to have a permanent residence on pre-TNIT planets or have interpersonal relationships with members of pre-TNIT civilizations.

If the law were to be repealed, the Union citizens would be able to visit and stay on any pre-TNIT planets without the Ministry's sanction. It would also mean that a marriage to a member of a pre-TNIT civilization would be recognized by the Union law.

However, experts think it is unlikely that the 156th law will be repealed. So far, only a quarter of the Lord Chancellors seem to be in favor of the proposal.

Calluvian Society Gossip
Intergalactic Union Date: 18768.122

Amid all the political talk in the past few months, it has gone largely unnoticed that Prince Harht'ngh'chaali of the Second Grand Clan has barely been seen in the society. The press officer of the Second Royal House informed us that Prince Harht had been pursuing studies and has little time for social life. However, our insiders have learned that Prince Harht barely leaves his rooms anymore. If the rumors are to be believed, he is ill and has been ill for a long time now. We at the Calluvian Society Gossip wish the young prince a quick recovery, but one cannot help but wonder why the Second Royal House is being so tight-lipped about Prince Harht's illness.

Calluvian Daily
Intergalactic Union Date: 18768.163

Breaking! The amendment to the Bonding Law passed!

Now, upon reaching the age of majority, any Calluvian can file a petition to dissolve the childhood bond. However, not all petitions will be necessarily approved.

Calluvian Society Gossip
Intergalactic Union Date: 18768.165

Scandal in the Second Royal House!

As we reported yesterday morning, Lady Leylen'shni'gul filed a petition to dissolve her bond to Prince Harht'ngh'chaali. At the time we thought the girl was mad, but in light of what we have just learned, we might revise our opinion.

Late last night, another petition was filed by a member of the Second Royal House: by none other than Crown Prince Ksar'ngh'chaali. Our Lord Chancellor wishes to break his bond to his bondmate, too!

Now, we would never speculate or imply that the two petitions are connected, but one wonders, what is the rush? Have Prince Ksar and the lovely Lady Leylen'shni'gul had a secret fondness for each other all these years? If that is the case, what about Prince Harht, who is rumored to be ill? One also wonders if the Third Royal House will take offence on behalf of the jilted Prince Seyn...

Calluvian Daily
Intergalactic Union Date: 18768.183

In all the uproar caused by the amendment to the Bonding Law, the approaching session of the Ministry has been almost forgotten. However, if the proposed bill regarding the repeal of the 156th law passes, the potential consequences will be as life altering as the amendment to the Bonding Law.

Calluvian Political Herald
Intergalactic Union Date: 18768.206

Breaking! The Pre-TNIT law is repealed by a very narrow margin!

When it started to seem that the opponents of the repeal would prevail, the Lord Chancellor of the Planet Stuxz had a change of heart and voted in support of the repeal.

"It suddenly occurred to me that the 156th law cannot continue existing in its current form," the Lord Chancellor said. "I'm still not entirely convinced that it needed a complete repeal, but perhaps I will make amendments to it and suggest a new, softer law in the next session of the Ministry."

His former allies were unimpressed by his sudden change of heart.

"I believe the voting was somehow rigged," Lord Chancellor Aimanu insisted. "There are telepaths among the Lords."

However, such suspicions were dismissed by the Ministry's security. "The Chamber of Lords is protected by the best shields in the galaxy. Neither electronic nor telepathic interference is possible. The results are legitimate."

Chapter 26

Chewing on his pasta, Jake looked across the table at Adam. "So are you taking Nick on a second date?" he said. He had been wondering about it all morning but hadn't had the chance to ask his friend. Adam hadn't mentioned his date with Nick at all.

Adam's fork paused. He looked up from his plate.

"Date?" he said mildly. "I fucked him. He was a decent lay. That's all. No dating was involved."

"Ah." Jake returned his gaze to his pasta. Dammit. He liked Nick and had hoped he would be different from all the other guys Adam had hooked up with. So much for that.

Jake suppressed a sigh. He couldn't say he liked how coldly promiscuous his friend had become in the past year. Sure, Adam had never had trouble getting laid, but he'd never been the "fuck 'em and leave 'em" type. Adam used to get to know his sex partners at least a little before hooking up with them. These days, Jake wasn't sure Adam bothered to learn the guy's name before fucking him.

And to think that all those months ago Jake had been relieved when Adam had finally gotten a grip and started going out and getting laid again. He'd thought it meant the old Adam was back. He couldn't have been more wrong.

Jake actually preferred the unshaven, depressed shell of a man Adam had been after the little shit had left him again to the cold-hearted cynical asshole Adam was now. At least back then, Adam had shown some actual emotion, even if it was rage, grief and pain. Now there was just nothing.

Jake could only curse the day Adam had met that kid. Even if Adam was truly over the lying little prick, as he insisted, it was obvious that relationship had left scars too deep for them to heal completely — to heal right.

It had been a year, for fuck's sake. Jake wanted his mate back. Because the man sitting opposite him wasn't his old friend, no matter how put-together he looked. The old Adam's eyes had never been so cold and cynical. The old Adam hadn't had the cruel edge this Adam did. The old Adam would have never used a nice guy like Nick as a meaningless fuck and then discarded him so easily.

Jake wanted his best mate back.

"Something on my face?" Adam said, wiping his mouth with a napkin.

"No," Jake said, pushing his plate away. "Let's go back or we'll be late."

Adam nodded and signaled to the waiter for the bill.

As they made their way toward the office, someone called out, "Adam!"

Jake and Adam stopped and turned. Jake suppressed another sigh when he saw who it was. George, the young intern who'd been making eyes at Adam all week.

"Hey," George said, smiling at Adam from under his eyelashes. "I was wondering if you were free tonight —"

"He's not," Jake cut him off when he saw that Adam was starting to nod.

"Later, kid," he said with a fake smile, grabbing Adam's arm and all but dragging him toward the office.

Except Adam wasn't an easy man to manhandle. He freed his arm from Jake's grip and shot him an annoyed look. "I'm not?"

Jake scowled. "That kid is half in love with you, man! You would've broken his heart."

"I'm not a monster or something."

Jake scoffed. "Of course not. You would've just fucked him and then kicked him out."

Adam pressed his lips together. "Maybe I wanted him."

"Right. You aren't even into blonds."

Adam pulled a cigarette out and lit it. Jake grimaced and told himself Adam was a grown man. If he wanted to die from lung cancer, it was his own fucking business. It was just one of the many bad habits Adam had picked up in the last year.

Adam took a long drag and let the smoke out slowly. "Maybe now I like them. People change."

"Yeah," Jake said. They certainly did.

"What?" Adam said, without looking at him.

"You said you were over him," Jake said.

Adam turned his head and looked him in the eye. There was no emotion whatsoever in his dark eyes. "Over who?"

Jake shook his head. Right.

Adam took another drag and glanced at his watch. "We should head back," he said and did just that.

Sighing, Jake followed him.

Chapter 27

Six hours later, as Adam let himself inside his flat, he wondered if he should have brought the little blond intern home after all, regardless of what Jake had said.

Dropping his briefcase on the floor, Adam sighed in annoyance. He wished Jake would finally get off his back. First Jake had nagged him constantly, trying to convince him to go out and get laid, and when Adam had done just that, Jake had started nagging him that he was doing it too often. It was fucking rich, considering that Adam had gotten laid all those months ago just to get Jake off his back, because apparently he needed to hook up with someone to prove that he was fine.

He was fine. His word should have been enough. He was fine back then and he was more than fine now. It had been a year. He was fine. It pissed him off that Jake kept implying that he still wasn't over Harry. Of course he was over Harry.

He barely even remembered the color of Harry's eyes. Or the way Harry smiled happily when he was delighted or excited about something. Or the way Harry curled into him, like a flower toward the sun.

Clenching his jaw, Adam loosened his tie. Harry had been a lying little shit who'd fucked him up so badly that it had taken him months to recover. He'd nearly lost his job over Harry. His mother had had to come to London and yell at him for being one depressed fuck before he finally got a grip.

It had been a year. A long, shitty year but a year that had changed him a great deal. Apparently time did heal all wounds. The pain and the lovesickness and the feeling of betrayal had long disappeared, leaving only cold rage and nothing else.

Adam removed his tie and started unbuttoning his shirt. He rolled his neck from side to side, trying to ease some of his tension. He was unzipping his fly when a tentative knock broke the silence in the flat.

Adam frowned and headed to the door.

He turned the lock, pushed the door open—and went very still.

Because in front of him stood Harry, his violet eyes wide and wary and hungry at the same time.

Something in him lurched.

He did forget the exact color of his eyes.

"Hello," Harry said.

How fucking dare he.

Adam shut the door in his face.

He leaned his forehead against it, trying to calm down. His entire body was shaking—with rage and something else—and he couldn't fucking *think*.

Harry was there. Harry was there.

Adam couldn't remember how many months he'd hoped that Harry would come back. Three? Four?

And now, a fucking year later, the little shit dared come back, looking all pretty and doe-like, and he expected Adam to... to do what, exactly?

What the fuck did he want?

Setting his jaw, Adam yanked the door open again.

Harry still stood on the other side, looking pale and dejected. It didn't seem he'd moved an inch.

"What do you want?" Adam said harshly, trying not to look Harry in the eye. It pissed him off that those eyes still had so much power over him, despite everything.

"I..." Harry said, blinking.

Seriously. He looked like a china doll, not a real man. How could he ever want that? Harry wasn't even all that handsome. He was cute and pretty, but objectively, his face was too strange to call it handsome.

"I..." Harry said, his voice hoarse and expression dazed.

Following Harry's gaze, Adam realized Harry was staring at his bare chest and half-opened fly. The raw need in his eyes was hard to mistake for anything else.

Adam laughed. "Seriously?"

He couldn't fucking believe it. "Is that what you came for? My cock?"

Harry flushed. "You d-don't understand."

"You're right: I don't," Adam bit off before turning around and heading to the couch. He sat on it and looked at Harry, who had followed him dazedly into the flat.

The little shit was still looking at his crotch, as if it held all the answers in the world. Cold rage bubbled through Adam's veins. He'd nearly drunk himself into oblivion because of Harry, but apparently all Harry wanted was his cock. Nice.

"Is that really what you came for?" Adam said and barely recognized his voice, so ugly it was.

Harry licked his lips. "I..."

"You know what?" Adam said, pulling his fly open. "Fine." Despite the rage inside him, he was hard. Of course he was when Harry was looking at his cock like he was gagging for it. If Harry had come for a quick, nasty fuck, who was he to deny him that? Maybe that would finally make him forget the last and only time they'd made love — had fucked. Had fucked. That was all it had been.

"You want my cock?" Adam leaned back against the couch, looking hard at Harry. "Come sit on it."

Harry literally *swayed* on his feet, his eyes still fixed on Adam's crotch. Christ, he looked almost drugged, his expression needy and his eyes glazed.

"I..." Harry said, taking a step to the couch, and then another. "We need to talk." And yet, despite his words, he was straddling Adam's lap and taking Adam's cock into his shaking hands.

Fuck. Adam took a breath through his gritted teeth, unable to believe Harry was actually doing this.

His hands twitched and he gripped the couch to stop himself from touching Harry. Fuck, he felt like a starved man forcing himself not to eat the feast laid out before him. The feast was only deceptively sweet. It was fucking poisonous. He'd barely put himself together last time. He wasn't doing it again.

Adam hissed as Harry squeezed his cock with both hands. "We r-really need to talk," Harry stuttered, sounding completely *out* of it, before suddenly whining and hiding his face in Adam's chest. "I'm sorry, I'm sorry — I can't — I need it too much."

He nuzzled his cheek into Adam's bare chest before latching onto his nipple and sucking hungrily, his hands stroking Adam's cock greedily. Adam bit his lip hard, his fingers burying in Harry's hair while Harry sucked on Adam's nipple like a hungry baby, moaning and writhing on Adam's lap, trying to wriggle out of his sweatpants—or at least what looked like sweatpants but was made of a strange smooth fabric.

Finally, Harry managed it and straddled his lap again, naked from below the waist, and ground his ass against his cock.

Adam hissed. Harry whined.

Adam bit the inside of his cheek, trying to regain some semblance of control. He should push Harry away and throw him out of his flat. He should, instead of thinking about where to get condoms and lube. But as he looked at Harry's flushed, dazed face, the harsh words that had been on the tip of Adam's tongue got stuck in his throat.

Before Adam realized what was happening, Harry was sinking down onto his cock.

Adam's eyes widened. He swore through his teeth. He was clean, but it was still irresponsible as hell. They shouldn't be doing this. They shouldn't be doing this for so many reasons. Good reasons. One of them being that fucking without lube was never a good idea.

"Wait, Haz—" But Harry wasn't dry. He was so fucking slick already, wet tightness enveloping his cock as Harry moaned, a wrecked expression on his face, pink lips slack and eyes glazed.

What the fuck.

How—why—

Adam tried to ask, tried to speak, tried to think, but all rational thought left his brain when Harry started riding him. All he could think about was Harry, Harry, Harry, and want, want, want.

He could only stare at Harry, feeling drugged and rendered speechless by the sight of him.

Harry was biting his lips, an almost pained expression on his face as he rode Adam clumsily, his breath coming in short, ragged gasps, his lovely thighs trembling with effort.

Their eyes met and locked.

"Adam," Harry said breathlessly, sliding his hands up Adam's chest and curling them around Adam's neck. "Please."

"What?" Adam croaked, feeling his barriers coming down one after another the longer Harry looked at him.

"Please," Harry said again, pulling Adam's head to his until their foreheads pressed together as he squirmed on Adam's cock. "Need you. I need you. I missed you."

Goddammit.

Adam bit at Harry's slack, panting mouth, and then again and again, until the biting kisses turned into wet, deep ones. Harry was moaning happily into his mouth, and Christ, Harry. Harry, Harry, Harry. Adam shoved Harry onto the couch and was on top of him before Harry's back even hit the couch. He pushed his cock back inside Harry's slick hole, eliciting a long, blissful moan from Harry. Propping himself on his elbows, Adam gave Harry what he wanted: he took.

Harry went absolutely crazy under him, clawing at Adam's back, his nails digging into his skin even through Adam's shirt and legs wrapping around Adam's hips, urging him on.

Adam didn't need to be urged on. He had never fucked anyone like this: as if he needed it in his blood, as if he'd die if he didn't get his cock deep enough into Harry, as if this was what he lived for. They both were moaning, the slick sound of his cock moving in and out of Harry's hole the only other sound in the room. The sex felt so fucking dirty in the best sense of the word.

Soon, Harry was sobbing, arching under him and mumbling something incoherent—something that didn't even sound like English.

"English, babe," Adam said, sucking hungry kisses into Harry's pale neck as he pounded into him.

"Please come in me," Harry mumbled, rolling his hips to meet Adam's thrusts. "Want you to come in me."

Adam shuddered, the weird request doing things to his primitive side. Fuck. He did want it. He wanted to come inside Harry, fill him up with his come until Harry's tummy was full of it and Harry continued leaking Adam's come for hours—

A groan ripped out of his throat as he started to come, staggered by the rush of pleasure. He was shoving deep into Harry with each wave of it, drawing it out into something overwhelming. Harry cried out, arching under Adam and sobbing in relief as he orgasmed, his hole clenching around Adam's softening cock.

Fuck.

Adam dropped his face beside Harry's, his limbs weak and his mind blissfully blank.

Chapter 28

They lay like that for a long time, sweaty bodies tangled on the couch.

Adam had no idea how much time had passed when he lifted his head and looked down at Harry's flushed, pleasure-struck face. So damn beautiful. So pretty. Harry.

A persistent thought niggled at the back of his mind, a sense that he had forgotten something, but it hovered on the edges of memory.

Adam frowned, finally remembering the most peculiar thing.

Reaching down, he touched the strange slick on Harry's inner thighs. It was colorless and scentless, similar to lube, but... Even if Harry had prepared himself before coming here—which was hard to believe—this stuff had *leaked* out of Harry non-stop. Adam distinctly remembered Harry getting slicker the longer they had fucked, which...shouldn't have been possible. It shouldn't have been fucking possible.

His brows furrowed, Adam lifted his eyes to Harry, not sure what to think.

Harry was looking at Adam warily. "I..." he said. "I can explain. I'm going to explain everything I couldn't explain before. I'll explain why I left."

Adam's lips thinned. He rolled off Harry and sat up. Now that his brain wasn't fuzzy with desire, he did remember that he was pissed off at Harry. But if Harry was really going to explain everything, he would hear him out.

"Go on," he said coldly.

"I..." Harry said, wringing his hands before looking down and flushing when he realized that he was naked from the waist down. Harry sat up and tugged his shirt down to cover his crotch. He cleared his throat and looked at Adam apprehensively.

"I'm an alien."

Christ, what an anticlimax.

Adam gave a harsh laugh. "It's not funny anymore." He had thought he was really getting an explanation. So much for that.

Harry frowned. "I'm not trying to be funny. I'm an alien. As in, from another planet. That's the truth."

"Right," Adam said. He couldn't believe Harry was reducing everything to a joke again instead of giving him an honest answer for once.

"I'm an alien," Harry insisted, a note of desperation creeping into his voice.

"Okay," Adam said, tucking himself in and zipping up his trousers. He was so damn sick of this.

"Adam!"

"What?" Adam bit out.

Harry smiled at him shakily. "I'm telling the truth. Look at my mouth. See? This is the proof that I'm telling the truth."

Adam scoffed. But then he stopped and stared.

Harry's mouth wasn't moving. And yet he could hear Harry's voice perfectly.

"I'm an alien. A telepathic alien," Harry's voice said as Harry's mouth didn't move an inch. *"That's why I couldn't stay with you. That's why I couldn't tell you much about me. I'll show you."*

Before Adam could even think what he could have possibly meant, there was an image of a green-and-blue planet in his mind. It looked a little like Earth, but it clearly wasn't. It was a lot greener, for one thing. It had only one continent, for another.

"This is my home planet," Harry's voice said in his mind before the image disappeared.

Adam shook his head slowly. He was seeing things. He must have been hallucinating. There was no other explanation.

Maybe he was dreaming and Harry wasn't even there.

"You are not dreaming, Adam," Harry said aloud, smiling at him uncertainly. "I'm really here."

Adam stared. "Are you reading my mind?"

Harry bit his thumb. "Sorry. I just wanted to prove to you I was telling the truth."

"And the truth is you're an alien," Adam said without any inflection.

Harry nodded with a hopeful look. "Do you believe me now?"

Adam stood, walked to the window and opened it, allowing the cool evening air into the room. He closed his eyes, trying to make sense of it all. A part of him was still certain this must have been a joke, that Harry was going to laugh any moment now and say he was kidding.

But he had heard Harry's voice in his mind. He had seen Harry's planet in his mind. Unless he was going insane, he would have to seriously consider the possibility that Harry was telling the truth—that he was an alien.

An alien.

Fuck, the mere idea was ridiculous, but Adam forced himself to consider it seriously.

An alien.

That would certainly explain a few things about Harry. More than a few things.

Adam bit the inside of his cheek as he thought about the fact that his MI6 friend couldn't find a person matching Harry's appearance in any country—or the fact that Harry seemed so completely oblivious about most basic things any human would just know. Or the fact that Harry had always been shady when he talked about his home and his family. Or the fact that Harry apparently produced natural slick when he was aroused. Or the fact that the bones in Harry's knee were oddly shaped. Or the fact Harry had the most unusual porcelain skin that didn't even seem human at times. Or the fact that Harry's hair had always seemed silky-smooth. Or the fact that Harry had very unusual violet eyes. Or the fact that Harry had always been unusually passionate about aliens and the way they were portrayed in the media.

Or the fact that Harry had literally told him he was an alien after they had met.

Adam opened his eyes and turned around. "Please tell me you aren't actually from a star system in the Sagittarius constellation," he said with a pinched look.

Harry gave him a sheepish smile. "No? We don't call it Sagittarius."

"But you're really an alien from the Sagittarius constellation," Adam said tonelessly.

Harry nodded. "We don't call it that," he said again. "Stars look different from different planets."

"We," Adam repeated. "Who is that?"

Harry cocked his head to the side and eyed him warily. "Calluvians," he said. "Or to be precise, Cal'luv'vians, but the planet's name was standardized when we became part of the Union of Planets, because most other races couldn't even hear the whole word—" Harry cut himself off. "Sorry. I'm babbling. It's probably not interesting to you. Are you really taking it well or are you going to do this thing humans often do when you laugh for no reason?"

"I don't know," Adam said with a crooked smile. "Probably."

Harry pouted. "I thought you believed me."

Sighing, Adam raked his hand through his hair. "You do realize how insane all of this sounds, right?"

He pinched the bridge of his nose. "Okay, let's say I believe you. You're an alien. Great. What are you doing here?"

"Here?" Harry looked around and then down at his half-naked body Adam was trying hard not to look at.

He couldn't afford to be distracted. It was already hard enough to wrap his mind around all of this.

"On Earth," Adam clarified before chuckling. "Are we being invaded or something?"

Harry gave him a disappointed look. "I really don't understand why humans are so fixated on the notion of aliens being interested in invading you. I thought I told you my thoughts on this."

"Ah, yes," Adam said, not without sarcasm. "I remember us discussing the totally hypothetical subject of aliens."

Harry, to his credit, had the grace to look ashamed.

"I never wanted to lie to you," he said quietly. "I just couldn't tell you anything. There are laws, you know. Earth hasn't yet reached the technological and cultural level required for Contact."

Adam suppressed the urge to look around for some hidden cameras.

Despite the telepathy, despite everything Harry had told him, a part of him still couldn't believe that what Harry was telling him was real.

Harry—the cute, quirky guy he'd met at the coffee shop and fallen in love with—couldn't possibly be an alien.

Aliens were supposed to be ugly, with big gray heads and creepy black eyes.

Aliens were supposed to be evil and creepy, not... not kind and ridiculously endearing.

His Harry couldn't be an alien.

His Harry.

Harry.

"You said your name was really Harry," Adam said, closing his eyes for a moment. "Was that another lie?"

Harry shook his head. "You could say it's a nickname for my name. I liked it so much that I told my family to call me Harry. It is my name now. I swear."

"And what is your given name, then?"

Harry pulled a face. "Humans can't pronounce it. I'm not sure you'll even hear all of it."

Leaning back against the windowsill, Adam crossed his arms over his chest. "So what is it?"

He caught Harry's eyes lingering on the muscles of his arms and chest and nearly laughed when his cock twitched in response to the appreciation in Harry's eyes. Bloody hell. Harry was telling him he was an alien, but apparently his body didn't give a damn.

Harry said something softly. It sounded like music.

"What?" Adam said.

Harry repeated it slower, "Harht'ngh'chaali. That's my full name."

Adam's brows furrowed. That was quite a mouthful. "And what does it mean?"

"Well, Harht is my first name, I guess, though not really. It's hard to explain it in human terms. Chaali is the name of my clan. The 'ngh' means... high, I guess."

"High?" Adam said.

Harry shrugged. "Some things are hard to translate. I guess you could say it means royal or noble, maybe." Harry frowned, looking pretty frustrated with his inability to explain it.

Adam blinked slowly. "Royal?"

Harry scrunched up his nose. "My mother is a queen."

"A queen," Adam repeated. "As in, the queen of the planet?"

"No!" Harry said with a laugh.

Thank fuck.

"Our planet has twelve grand clans," Harry said. "Which are like kingdoms, I suppose." He frowned again. "Sometimes the translating chip is so useless. I would never call our grand clans kingdoms, but that's what it comes up with as the next best thing."

"The translating chip?"

"Yeah, it's a chip we have under our skin. Our chips are connected to our brains and help us learn foreign languages quickly, but it's not faultless." Harry chuckled. "You should have seen how I sounded the first day on Earth! No one could understand me! But by the third day, I finally got pretty good at your language."

"You learned English in three days?" Adam said. For some reason, that was more mind-boggling than anything else.

Harry nodded. "My parents always said I had a natural knack for languages," he said, not without pride, and smiled.

Adam wondered how it was possible to be so angry at someone and also be so endeared by them at the same time.

Inwardly, he laughed at himself. Apparently even the fact that Harry was an alien didn't change a thing. A year apart, and he still had it as bad.

A year.

"It's been a year, Harry," Adam said. "Why did you leave? Why come back now?"

"I don't know where to start," Harry said slowly.

"From the beginning would be good."

Harry chewed on his lip. "Long story short, my parents originally sent me to Earth as punishment for my misdemeanor. I used my familiar link to my sister to learn her secret and was caught. Technically, it was a crime. My parents were angry. They sent me to Earth to 'learn some responsibility.'" Harry looked at him. "You have to understand that I couldn't tell you that I was an alien. There are—were—laws forbidding it. I told you the truth: the first time I left, my parents simply had me transported back without any warning."

"And you couldn't even say goodbye?"

Harry shook his head. "I didn't know they were going to teleport me back. The TNIT— transgalactic teleporter— takes just a few seconds. It locked on my identification chip and transported me back."

Adam gave him a pinched look.

Harry's shoulders sagged in defeat. "You don't believe me."

"I do," Adam said with a sigh. "It's just pretty hard to wrap my mind around aliens, teleporters, identification chips and..." He shook his head. "Go on. So your parents transported you back. Why did you return? With that friend of yours?"

"I told you—Seyn helped me get here. My parents had forbidden me to go back to Earth. And legally, I couldn't visit a pre-TNIT planet more than once a year. So Seyn had to ask his friend from another planet to sneak us in."

"And why did Seyn tag along?" Adam said.

Harry pulled a face. "He wanted to get rid of his bond."

"His bond?"

"It's a long story," Harry said. "I could show you, if you would like? It would be faster and easier. I promise I won't pry into your thoughts."

Adam studied the earnest expression on his face. After some hesitation, he nodded stiffly.

Harry beamed at him. "Just look me in the eye."

Adam braced himself, but he still wasn't prepared for the sudden onslaught of thoughts and memories that weren't his.

Fuck.

There was so much information on Harry's culture, on the bond thing, on how it limited Harry's race's senses and hindered their telepathy.

"Wait," Adam said, blinking and interrupting the flood of information. "You used your telepathy on humans? To trick them?"

"It was just those few times," Harry said defensively. "Seyn and I didn't have any documents or money to get from Los Angeles to London."

"Have you ever used your telepathy on me?"

"No!" Harry said.

Adam eyed him. His heart insisted that Harry would never do it to him, but the sheer force of that belief made him wary.

"I've always wanted you too much," Adam said slowly. "Wanted to protect you and take care of you from the moment I saw you. I always thought it was bloody strange how badly I wanted to protect a bloke I barely knew. You always felt like mine, even back then. It was so unlike me to fall for someone so hard and so fast."

Harry blushed and looked very pleased for a moment before frowning and shaking his head. "I swear I didn't influence you in any way. I swear, Adam."

Clenching his jaw, Adam looked away. "Go on," he said. "So you came back the first time because your friend wanted to break his bond."

"And because I missed you," Harry said.

Adam pursed his lips. "And then what? Your brother found you and took you both back? You couldn't convince him to let you stay?"

"I couldn't stay. He found out about our relationship and was furious that I put our family at such risk."

"What risk?" Adam said tersely. He still wasn't sure he believed that Harry had never influenced him in any way. He wanted to believe Harry. He wanted it too much. That made him wary.

He couldn't help but remember Jake's words. *I don't get what you see in him. He's cute, yeah, but there are plenty of cute boys out there. I've never seen you so gone over a bloke before.*

"Ksar was angry, because I broke several intergalactic and Calluvian laws," Harry replied, tearing Adam away from his thoughts. "I couldn't stay on Earth. Sooner or later, I would have been found, and the ramifications for my entire family wouldn't have been pretty. Legal trouble aside, my family's social and political standing would have been destroyed if anyone found out about us."

"Why?" Adam said, bristling. "I know we humans don't have fancy identification chips and teleporters, but we're hardly barbarians."

"I know. *I* know that. But..." Harry pulled a face. "My species can be a bit... arrogant."

"Yes," Adam said. "I met your brother."

Harry winced. "Ksar can be a little high-handed, but he's a good person deep down."

Somehow, Adam doubted it.

"It still doesn't change the fact that you left because of fucking politics," he said. He didn't know whether to laugh or rage.

"It's not that simple," Harry said, a look of concern flashing through his face. "The political landscape on my planet is very shaky. There's a growing faction of telepathically null politicians trying to overthrow telepaths from the grand clans' thrones."

"I thought all of your race was telepathic," Adam said.

Harry shook his head. "Telepathically null Calluvians aren't entirely non-telepathic like you. They have some passive ability—they can have bonds and familial links—but they're pretty much useless. They can't use their telepathy actively, so they're not classified as telepaths. The t-nulls used to be a minority, but in the last couple of centuries they have become the majority."

His brows furrowed. "There's a real concern that they might overthrow the current royal families. They just need an excuse to do it. If I remained unbonded, if I remained a Class 3 telepath, I would have been declared dangerous and they would have used my case to prove that telepaths aren't suited for positions of power. So I went home with Ksar before anyone found out." Harry looked at him imploringly. "Please say something."

Adam walked to the mini bar and opened a bottle of whiskey. "So you always knew we had an expiration date. Must be nice."

He didn't try to soften his voice. He wasn't in the mood to spare Harry's feelings. He felt used in the worst possible way. While he was falling for Harry, Harry had always known they had no future.

"I—"

"Why are you here, then?" Adam bit off and took a swig of whiskey. "To fuck me, fuck me up again, and then go back to your top-lofty planet? What happened to wishing me happiness and new love?" He laughed, thinking about the note Harry had left.

He hated the fucking thing.

Hated it for knowing it by heart.

"I never thought I'd be back," Harry said quietly. "I thought I'd never see you again. When I returned home, Ksar restored my bond to my bondmate before anyone could find out. I thought I could learn to live with it again. But I... I was wrong."

Something in Harry's voice made Adam turn around.

Harry was looking down at his hands. "Please don't think badly of my brother. He's not a bad person. If it weren't for him, I wouldn't be here. I'm here only because Ksar worked so hard to make it possible." Harry caught his bottom lip between his teeth, hesitation flickering on his face. "If it weren't for Ksar, I could've died."

Adam felt his muscles tense up and had to consciously relax them. Harry was there. Harry was fine.

"What do you mean?"

Harry pressed his cheek against the back of the couch, his lashes hiding his expression. "A few thousand years ago, there was a planet-wide war on Calluvia. Some truly terrible biological weapons were used. By the time the war ended, the population was mostly sterile. Our geneticists solved it, but the experimental genetic therapy had unexpected side effects."

"I know," Adam said. He had seen something about it when Harry had explained the bond thing in his mind. "You said it caused telepathic mutations."

Harry nodded. "Not only. Some mutations were physical. After the gene therapy, there started being born babies that shared a specific gene with our long extinct ancestor, the surl'kh'tu." Harry looked at Adam. "I have the gene."

Adam was starting to get a bad feeling. "And?"

Harry shrugged, looking mildly flustered. "It's different for all of us, but usually it means that people with the gene—we call them throwbacks—are biologically equipped to have sex with either gender."

Adam's forehead wrinkled. It seemed bizarre, but it did explain why Harry produced natural lubrication. "What does it have to do with your nearly dying?"

Harry brushed a hand through his hair. "Every throwback is different. Some share more traits with the surl'kh'tu while others are barely different from modern Calluvians. It was theorized for centuries that if it weren't for the bond binding us to a specific person, throwbacks might have retained other aspects of our ancestor's biology." Harry blushed. "Like the fact that after their first mating, the surl'kh'tu started needing their mate physically. It was supposedly a natural mechanism that ensured procreation, because they mated for life."

Harry swallowed and said quietly, "Some time after I got home, I started feeling off. Everything felt wrong. I felt wrong. Empty." Harry rubbed his chest absentmindedly, as if chasing away a lingering phantom ache. "I don't know if I would've really died, but I was losing my mind. To be honest, I don't really remember the last few months all that well. Everything was a blur. I couldn't think. I just needed you."

Adam bit the inside of his cheek. "What you're describing sounds like an illness." Illness, not feelings.

"It was, sort of."

Right. Harry hadn't come back because he missed him. He'd come back because of some biological imperative.

Adam took another swig of whiskey.

Oblivious to the sick feeling in Adam's stomach, Harry continued, "Ksar restored my bond to Leylen'shni'gul, but it didn't feel the same. It could suppress my senses, but it couldn't suppress my biology. When Ksar realized I had to go back to you, he launched political campaign not only on our planet but also in the Ministry—"

"How nice of him," Adam said, looking at the bottle in his hand. "Now get out."

Silence.

"What?" Harry whispered.

"You heard me," Adam said. He knew his voice sounded cold and mean. He made no attempt to change it. "Get out. You got what you came here for. Now get out."

He could hear Harry inhale and exhale shakily. "Did you—do you not want me anymore?"

Adam brought the bottle to his lips. "Of course I want you," he said, intentionally misunderstanding Harry's words. He looked Harry in the eye. "I fucked you, didn't I?"

Harry's mouth fell open.

A small wrinkle appeared between his brows. "You're being mean," he said, looking more puzzled than hurt. "You're not mean."

Adam took a small swig from the bottle. "People change. That's life. You should go. It's been a long day. I'm knackered."

Harry stared at him.

"What?" Adam said. "Your ride isn't here yet? The teleporter has to recharge? Sorry, I'm just a barbarian human, good only for fucking. I have no idea how your sophisticated technology works."

Harry cocked his head to the side, studying him like a bird. A very pretty bird he wanted to kiss all over.

Adam closed his eyes for a moment. For fuck's sake.

"Get out," he grated out, angrier at himself than at Harry.

He didn't watch Harry leave.

He felt it more than he heard it when Harry left.

Adam looked around the quiet living room. It didn't look any different. It didn't look darker or emptier. It didn't make him feel lonely. It didn't make him feel anything.

He felt nothing.

Adam dropped himself on the couch and brought the bottle to his lips again, looking at the ceiling without really seeing it.

He could remember the day he had met Harry so clearly. The funny thing was, he usually went to the coffee shop around the corner and never went to the coffee shop Harry worked at—he didn't like it much. If his favorite coffee shop hadn't been so crowded that day, he would have likely never met Harry.

He wished he never had.

Adam took another swig from the bottle, relishing the burn, and then another.

He paused with the bottle at his lips when the door slammed open. Harry marched back in, an uncharacteristically mulish expression on his face.

"I won't let you do this," Harry said, striding to Adam.

Adam could only stare at him. Before he regained the ability to speak, Harry straddled his lap and pinned Adam's shoulders to the back of the couch with his hands. Adam could have easily pushed him off.

He was just too stunned to move.

"I refuse to believe you don't feel anything for me anymore," Harry said, looking in his eyes intently. "I know you still feel something. I felt it. I felt it during sex."

Adam put on a blank face. "Sex is just sex. Don't misunderstand it for something else. You told me to get over you. I have."

Harry's lip wobbled. "You're lying. You're just hurt that I lied to you. I didn't want to. I'm sorry. I'm really, really sorry."

Jesus fucking Christ. Those eyes should have been outlawed. Of course they were inhuman.

"I don't want your apologies," he said coldly. He told himself it was the right thing to do. Harry had never loved him the way Adam loved him. Harry had come back only because of some biological imperative, for fuck's sake. Harry had lied to him for ages and nothing would stop him from lying to him again. Harry could disappear anytime he wanted, whenever he didn't need Adam's cock. Their relationship had always been too skewed, with Adam always waiting for Harry to come back and stay.

He had to cut his losses, no matter how much he wanted to wrap Harry in his arms, fill him up and swallow him whole, taste and mark and memorize every inch of him, hide him somewhere only he had access to, and breathe him in, always.

"I'm not lying," Adam said, looking Harry in the eye and hoping Harry wasn't reading his mind. "You told me to get over you. It's been a year. I got over you. Numerous times. I've been with other people."

The fact that he felt guilty about it proved how fucked up he still was over Harry.

He didn't owe Harry anything. Harry had used him and ditched him for his family, and had the nerve to tell Adam to be *happy* in a goddamn letter. He owed Harry nothing.

Harry's nostrils flared at Adam's words, his hands tightening on Adam's shoulders. "You didn't love any of them," he said, his voice thick and laden with possessiveness. "I'm your only babe. You told me so." Harry's voice broke a little and he stopped to take a deep breath. "I don't believe that you don't love me anymore. Please just tell me what made you upset. Maybe I can explain. I want to explain. I want to be with you."

Harry smiled shakily, looking at him with such longing and need in his eyes that Adam felt himself respond in more ways than one, against his better judgment.

Adam averted his gaze for a moment, trying to get control over his body and his emotions.

"What you feel for me isn't love, Harry," he said. "That's my main problem."

A look of confusion settled on Harry's face. "What?"

"You returned not because you loved me," Adam said flatly. "But because of some biological need I won't pretend to understand. Yes, you needed me. You needed my body. Where's the guarantee that you'll stay this time for good? I'm tired, Haz. I'm tired of feeling like shit whenever you disappear." He chuckled. "Now that I know you aren't even from this planet, it's way worse. If you disappear again, I can't even follow you. No one would tell me if something happened. Living in constant doubt and fear isn't fun."

Harry's hand traveled along Adam's jaw, soft against his stubble, his fingers running through the hair at the back of his neck. "I understand. Do you think I'm not scared? I am. You're a completely different species. I need you, but you don't *need* me. I know you're it for me, but you don't. You might stop having feelings for me any moment." Harry's eyelashes lowered. "You have no idea what it's like to need someone the way I need you."

Adam laughed harshly and tipped Harry's chin up, forcing him to look him in the eye. "No idea? I dreamed about your smile even after I convinced myself that I hated you. I fucked other men and hated them—and hated myself for imagining you in their stead every goddamn time. I couldn't even go into your room for months without losing it. You might need me physically, but I want more. Needing isn't enough. You're here because of fucking biology. The truth is, if you didn't literally need me, you wouldn't have come back."

Harry stared at him for a long time before a broken, bitter laugh left his throat.

"I couldn't, Adam," he choked out. "Ksar wouldn't have helped me if my life and sanity weren't at stake." Harry shook his head. "You misunderstood it. The mating for life thing the surl'kh'tu did? It wasn't just biology. They weren't some kind of mindless animals. They were very selective, and after choosing their partner, they courted them for a long time. The studies proved that they couldn't even feel arousal if they didn't have emotional intimacy with their partner—their sexuality was similar to human demisexuality. Only once the surl'kh'tu mated physically, the biological imperative kicked in."

Harry smiled at him shakily. "I loved you and wanted to be yours long before we even had sex. It wasn't biology. It was all me. I just didn't understand completely what I wanted because of my bond." He chuckled, blushing. "Don't you remember how I was always all over you, wanting cuddles and hugs and your hands on me? I loved being close to you, loved your scent, even when you came from the gym and claimed that you smelled gross. I loved being your babe, your love, and your sweetheart."

Adam stared at him.

He didn't know what to think.

What to believe.

"I always loved touching you," Harry said softly, licking his lips. He moved his hands from Adam's shoulders and slipped them under Adam's unbuttoned shirt. "Even when I was incapable of feeling arousal, I was still attracted to you so badly I felt the attraction even despite the bond, but I couldn't quite understand what I felt until the bond broke completely."

Harry looked Adam in the eye, his face open and earnest. "I was ridiculously smitten with you. You were my sun and my moon and my stars. I wanted to make you happy. I wanted to impress you. I wanted you to smile at me and call me love. I wanted you to say I was special to you, your only babe. I fell in love with you long before I was even capable of feeling lust."

Harry took Adam's hand and brought it to his lips. "I love you," he murmured. "I always have. The fact that I need you physically doesn't negate the fact that I love you so very much. Because I do."

Adam bit the inside of his cheek.

Harry nuzzled into his hand like a kitten. "I love you. I love you more than you can imagine. I don't care what people back home will think of me because of our relationship. I want to be yours. I *am* yours. Your Harry." Harry kissed Adam's palm, looking at him with open longing in his eyes. "Yours. For as long as you'll have me."

Adam could only look at him, his heart pounding. "Really?" he said, his lips barely moving.

His eyes shiny, Harry nodded. "You are all I dream about. I want to grow old with you. I want to kiss your wrinkles when they appear. I want to have kids with your eyes and your smile someday and spoil them rotten. I want forever." Harry kissed the inside of Adam's wrist, sending goosebumps up his arm.

Adam licked his lips, trying to shake off the fog of want that started to cloud his mind again. He frowned as something occurred to him. Harry had said he had throwback traits of his ancestor who had been intersex. "Wait. You can't actually get pregnant, right?"

Harry burst out laughing, hiding his face in Adam's shoulder. "No! I'm male. I have some biological traits of the surl'kh'tu, but I can't actually conceive." He paused, a wrinkle appearing on his forehead. "Well, I'm pretty sure of it."

"He says he's pretty sure," Adam said dryly, amused despite himself. After all the stuff Harry had told him, male pregnancy wouldn't have been the most shocking.

Harry smiled at him, his eyes a little moist as they searched Adam's. "So do you forgive me? Do you believe me?" Harry swallowed. "You still love me, right?" His voice cracked a little, and Adam couldn't.

He couldn't keep fighting it anymore.

He crushed Harry in his arms, hugging him tightly and burying his face in his chestnut hair. "Of course I do, Haz," he murmured, his throat thick with emotion. "I never stopped and don't think I ever will." He kissed Harry on the temple. "I love you, baby."

He felt Harry smile against his shoulder before Harry lifted his head.

"Babe," he corrected Adam with a grin before slotting their mouths together.

Adam laughed and kissed him.

Epilogue

Harry was fast asleep when there was a quiet knock on the door.

Adam was tempted to ignore it, reluctant to extricate himself from Harry's embrace, but the knocking didn't stop.

Adam brushed his lips against Harry's. Harry smiled in his sleep. Adam forced himself to pull away, giving Harry a pillow to hug in his stead. A little frown appeared on Harry's face, as if he wasn't fooled by the replacement, but eventually his breathing evened out again.

Adam slipped into a shirt and a pair of sweatpants before heading for the door.

His relaxed mood changed immediately when he saw the man who stood on the other side.

"You aren't taking him away," Adam said, blocking the doorway. He knew his voice was tight and cutting. He didn't care what Harry had said; this man was the one who'd taken Harry away from him, the reason Adam hadn't seen him for a year.

Ksar's strange silver eyes met his. They were impossible to read. "I'm the one who delivered him here. Did you think I would let him go to this planet alone in his state? He was barely coherent. He could barely walk or talk."

Adam had to remind himself Harry was fine now. Harry was sleeping in his bed, healthy and happy. Harry was fine. Harry was his.

"He's better now," Adam said, his voice clipped. "You can return to your planet." Even saying that was still fucking strange. "I'll take care of him." *He's mine to take care of.*

Ksar looked him in the eye and said nothing.

"Get out of my head," Adam said, accentuating every word.

Ksar didn't look fazed in the least. He nodded. "I've already seen everything I needed to see." He turned to leave but stopped and looked back. "He'll be with you for the time being. The political situation on our planet is very unstable right now. I'll come back for him when everything settles."

Adam went rigid, his fists clenching.

"He has a home and a family," Ksar said. "The scandal will die down eventually. He can't hide here forever. It's going to be difficult, but he *will* be reintegrated back into the society. He's a scion of kings, not a coffee shop boy."

Adam met his gaze dead-on. "I'm not letting you take him away again."

"I won't take him away from you—if you keep treating him right."

Ksar smiled. The smile didn't quite touch his eyes. "You don't want to know what I'll do to you if you don't."

Adam shot him an unimpressed look. "You don't need to threaten me. If you just read my mind, you know I'd kill for him." He wasn't even exaggerating.

"I know," Ksar said. "If I didn't, I wouldn't leave him here." For the first time in their short acquaintance, Ksar gave him a look that almost passed for friendly. Almost. "Make him happy," he said stiffly.

"I will," Adam said.

Ksar nodded and touched his own wrist. Immediately, a strange, nearly transparent fog swept over him, thickening into an impenetrable white blur.

And then he was gone.

Adam stared at the empty spot Ksar had just been and then chuckled. Fucking aliens. He couldn't believe this was his life now.

His mind was still reeling as he crawled back into bed.

Harry mumbled sleepily, "Who is it?"

Adam gathered him into his arms. "Your brother," he said, his fingers stroking the smooth skin of Harry's back. "He's already left."

Harry blinked his eyes open and peered at him. "You look off. Was he an ass?"

"No." Adam gave a chuckle. "I just… I saw him literally vanish into thin air, Harry. Like, actually seeing it… made it all real, I guess."

Frowning, Harry bit his thumb. "Does it bother you? That I'm not human—that I'm an alien?"

Adam laughed.

"I don't understand," Harry said with the cutest pout. "It's a serious question. Why are you laughing at me?"

"Because the answer should be obvious." Adam met Harry's eyes steadily. "Haz, I don't give a damn if you're a coffee shop boy or a prince from another planet." He leaned in and kissed Harry's nose and then his soft pink lips. God, he fucking adored him. "You're Harry. You're mine. That's all I care about."

"I like this answer," Harry said, burying his fingers in Adam's hair and kissing him back hard.

They kissed for what felt like hours until Adam felt nearly dizzy with love and want and happiness, and Harry was panting and whispering breathlessly *I love you* between the kisses. Fuck, this was... insane. This feeling.

"So," he said hoarsely, looking into Harry's glazed eyes. "I'm curious. Are there really aliens with large gray heads and creepy black eyes?"

Harry sighed.

"I have a confession to make," he said hesitantly. "That's actually what we really look like. We just mess with humans' minds and make you think that we look like you. It's an illusion."

Adam stared at him.

A giggle escaped Harry's lips before he burst out laughing.

"You little shit!" Adam jumped on top of him and started tickling him. They rolled around on the bed, laughing and then kissing again. Fuck, he couldn't get enough.

When they finally stopped laughing, Adam pressed their foreheads together.

"How do I say 'I love you so much' in your language? Asking for a friend."

Harry chuckled. "Your friend will never be able to pronounce it," he murmured, rubbing his nose against Adam's. He gave Adam a small, happy smile. "But tell him it doesn't matter."

Perhaps it didn't.

The End

About the Author

Alessandra Hazard is the author of the bestselling MM romance series *Straight Guys* and *Calluvia's Royalty*.

Visit Alessandra's website to learn more about her books: http://www.alessandrahazard.com/books/

To be notified when Alessandra's new books become available, you can subscribe to her mailing list: http://www.alessandrahazard.com/subscribe/

You can contact the author at her website or email her at author@alessandrahazard.com.

Printed in Poland
by Amazon Fulfillment
Poland Sp. z o.o., Wrocław

31180862R00147